Regretfully

Yours

B.L. Berg

Contents

Also by B.L. Berg:

Lady and the Tramp and Me

The Dream Maker and the Candy Cane

About the Author

B.L. Berg is a visionary author whose novels are a testament to her boundless imagination and storytelling prowess. With a racing mind, Berg finds inspiration in every corner of life, transforming the ordinary into the extraordinary with her words.

Her journey as a storyteller began long ago, marked by a tattoo above her heart that proudly declares her as such. Fuelled by her insatiable passion for narrative, Berg's tales are woven with depth, emotion, and a touch of magic that captivates readers from start to finish. Each story is a testament to her unique voice and her unwavering commitment to pushing the boundaries of traditional storytelling.

Follow B.L. Berg on:

Instagram.com/BLBergAuthor

Facebook.com/ BLBergAuthor

Twitter.com/BLBergAuthor

Newsletter sign-up: BLBergAuthor.com

CHAPTER 1

Regret

Ryan

Do you know what regret feels like? I do. It's not necessarily associated with guilt or shame, as you might think. No. Regret is manifested in a broken nose and a godawful lot of pain because your eyebrow is cracked, too, because the woman responsible – even when drunk – hits like she's bloody Katie Taylor.

Before I got back to my hometown, I thought regret was personified by a beautiful blonde woman. Graceful like an elf, tall, slim, elegant – almost ethereal. The skirt of the silky pastel dress flows behind her, and her hair blows lightly in the breeze even when she's inside. Claudia. The one I left behind when I was stationed abroad for a year as a part of an international exchange programme in the company where I work. I thought she would come with me, but she didn't. I thought she would miss me or at least think about me, but she didn't. She got engaged to another man.

So, for almost a year, while I've been away, I was under the impression that regret equalled Claudia – leaving her behind in particular. But I was wrong because that's not regret at all. Regret is a five-foot-one hellraiser who can do shots like an alcoholic and hit like a boxer. This one also bites, but I'm told it's only during sex. At least that's something – and absolutely none of my concern. So, judging by my smashed face, regret equals Daphne the Hellraiser. If that doesn't sound wrong, I don't know what does. If you've seen "Bridgerton", you know that's what a Daphne is *supposed* to look like. The Bridgerton Daphne might have punched Nigel Berbrooke, but honestly, I look more like poor Nigel after the Duke of Hastings got through with him.

Daphne, aka "Hellraiser", aka "Regret", aka "Hellhound in Human Form", is the little sister to the woman I thought was Regret, Claudia. Where Claudia is tall and graceful, Daphne is short and apparently forceful. She is pale like Claudia, but on Daphne it looks unhealthy and not delicate. She has short nails, a few freckles, and pink and blue hair – she lost a bet – that's starting to grow back to its normal boring brownish colour. Claudia would never make a bet like that – one that makes her look somewhat like a tie-dye experiment gone horribly wrong. Before Daphne broke my nose and almost knocked me out, I heard one of the other patrons at the pub say she had two more weeks of semi-blue/pink hair before she could change it.

I'm not *that* fond of the town I grew up in, but since Claudia still lives here, that doesn't leave me much of a choice. Because she's the reason I'm here. I have two months off from work and plenty of time and opportunity to win her back.

Where other towns may have a Christmas market as the highlight of their year, this town has the summer season. Summer in this town is the party season, just like it was in the Regency era. Pathetic really.

Picnics, weddings, sailing, softball matches, even dog's birthdays – almost any reason to eat too much, drink, dance, and be with family and friends and throw a party.

Also, during the summer season, the older generation, who is bored and ignored most of the year, is allowed to act like they're still human beings because they are invited to every picnic, wedding, dog's birthdays and so on. The rest of the year, they're left to their own devices, and their families pretend they're already dead and not just rotting away at the retirement home. They spend most of that time in endless discussions about what our town should be called. The town started as a farm, then two farms, then three, but nobody bothered naming it. What was once houses in between two villages are now a small town where the seniors are fighting for the town's own name and independence. Needless to say, it's a fruitless endeavour. Half of them are senile and can't even remember their own opinion for even two minutes, and none of them can agree upon the name. The only thing they agree on is that it has to be something with a "puddle". No matter where you go there's a muddy puddle you can't help stepping in. If you are smart, you might dress up for the festivities going on in the town, but until you arrive at your destination, you wear your wellies. Another problem is there already exists a Puddletown further South and it even has a local manor! We don't. Nobody will accept being either "Northeast Puddletown" or "New Puddletown". This town is actually much larger, but the small-town mentality is exactly that … small-minded.

One of the local farmers suggested Butterpuddle. He's a dairy farmer, of course, and he had hired a marketing agency – which was actually his cousin – to make a full-scale presentation with a brand-new logo for his butter and other products. My guess is he was hoping the seniors in town would be so thrilled about the idea they would invest their measly pensions in promoting his newly acquired trademark. They didn't. The logo was terrible; the cow looked like it was, in fact, a bull with huge balls, and the butter made it look like it had just ejaculated all over a piece of toast. Besides, Butterpuddle sounds disgusting – even before the logo.

Some from the older generation actually called the village "Mudpuddletown" until a charitable person told them what *mudpuddle* means in slang before they spent their pension on a large, new sign for the town.

I wish I'd been there that afternoon when the vicar's wife – who used to be a schoolteacher – had to explain to the old villagers that their suggestion could mean a wet, sloppy vagina or anal discharge. It must've been worse than *any* story *ever* told about the birds and the bees. So, the town is still without a name, but we've got a new vicar because all of a sudden, the seniors didn't like his wife very much.

She doesn't teach any more either because she is now considered to be some sort of deviant. Poor woman. Honestly, she should just have pretended not to know the meaning of the word and let the seniors name the bloody place "Mudpuddletown".

My parents live in one of the larger old limestone houses in town. That fortunately means I have a place to stay while I'm here getting Claudia back. Unlike in the movies, where parents keep their children's rooms intact, my mother could be a professional decorator, and I have to say I'm not at all sorry about that. My old room has been turned into something that could easily pass for the perfect B&B accommodation. It's a bit too romantic for my taste, but I'm only going to sleep here, and I'm certain Claudia will love it when I bring her home with me. I only hope my parents have toned their bedroom activities down a bit during the years because I'm certain not even the prettiest room in the world can make up for listening to *that*. In my childhood, they could be quite noisy and neither I nor my older brother Myles have recovered from hearing what goes on in my parents' bedroom. We've silently agreed never to mention it. Ever.

But so far, my return to town hasn't been the grand success I'd expected it would be. I got punched yesterday by Daphne, and this morning, my boss called – meaning I've been working all day. That was not supposed to happen. I wasn't supposed to get punched yesterday either, and in addition to the broken nose, the result is a swollen, black eye and a headache. "Good thing" I've only worked about ten hours in front of the computer today – with one eye. My head has been pounding all day, and I think I've swallowed about a year's supply of Ibuprofen. Bloody Daphne.

I make my way downstairs at a quarter to six. Dinner at my parent's house is at six-fifteen, and if you're not there, you go hungry. It's always been that way, and there's no reason to be fooled by the romantic décor in my old room – my mother could blend in at the strictest boarding schools in the country or in the military. She's also very caring and loving, but any kind of tardiness is not accepted.

"What happened?" my mother squeals as soon as I enter the open-plan kitchen. Yes, that's right, the woman with the almost military bearing can squeal like a teenage girl.

"Went to the pub last night," I mumble and gently rub my swollen eye.

"And got a welcome home present, it looks like," my father grumbles from behind the newspaper. My older brother Myles snickers.

"Why are you even here?" I ask him. He has his own flat on the outskirts of town, so there's no reason for him to be here, really.

"Why, to welcome you home, little brother," he says, grinning. I discreetly salute him with two fingers to show my opinion about that statement and he smiles, obviously very content he's being an annoying prick as always. My mother frowns at both of us.

"Why don't the two of you go into the library and have a drink," she suggests. Only it's not a suggestion. It's an order. She's probably hoping we'll get the snarliest remarks out of the way before we all sit down at the dinner table.

"The library" sounds very posh and fancy, but it's not. It's a tiny sitting room that only has room for a single bookcase and two Chesterfield armchairs in peacock blue velvet with high backs. Between them, there is a ramshackle yellow tile table my mother found at a flea market. It makes an odd combination, to say the least.

Myles pours two glasses of whiskey while I slump in one of the chairs.

"So, tell me," he says.

"Tell you what?"

"Tell me why you've returned. I thought you were never ever coming back."

"I missed you."

"Come on, Ryan," he groans like he doesn't believe a word I'm saying. He's right not to. I'm blatantly lying.

"I'm here to get her back."

"Who?"

"Claudia," I say with fierce determination. He raises both eyebrows so high I think they must be stuck at the back of his neck by now.

"Are you really that stupid?"

"It's not stupid." *It might be stupid.*

"And who hit you?" Myles asks and ignores my denial.

"Daphne." My brother roars with laughter, and since he hasn't yet taken a sip of whiskey he can choke on, I seriously hope he strains something that will give him a lot of pain – preferably permanently. Then I could lock him up in a retirement home at the ripe age of thirty-two, and I wouldn't even bat an eye doing it.

When he eventually stops laughing, he actually has to wipe his eyes. He is such a bastard.

"Why did she hit you?"

"She said she hates me and can't stand the sight of me." He nods like he's in agreement – and I wouldn't put it past him.

"Understandable," he says with a thoughtful nod and confirms my suspicion. He finally takes a sip of his whiskey, but unfortunately, he doesn't choke.

"Fuck off, Myles," I grumble.

"Seriously, I understand Daphne. Each and every time Claudia breaks up with someone, it's like the world's end. Strangely, you were no exception. Poor thing."

"Claudia?"

"No, Daphne, of course. Imagine being forced to watch that time and time again. Like a school play that won't go away." He shivers visibly while I, on the other hand, smile happily. Myles was a cloud once in a play at school. I don't quite remember what it was called, but it was something about a gardener and a sprout growing. Unfortunately for him, our uncle recorded the whole sordid affair with Myles singing the *Drippy Song* with two of his friends as fellow clouds. There's been a lot of jokes and a lot of anonymous adult diaper deliveries throughout the years because of that. I'm only responsible for about half of them.

"Daphne doesn't deserve pity, *Drippy*."

"She runs the pub, you know?" he says and ignores my barbed remark about his disgraceful past as a singing cloud.

"No, I didn't." Claudia has always appreciated nice men and getting a black eye and broken nose in the pub, no less, does *not* fall into that category. I never should have ventured to the pub and by God, I regret it. Bloody Daphne!

"Gavin still owns it, but he's as lazy as he's ever been."

"Explains why he let his employee hit me," I grumble. I seriously doubt it would've been any less humiliating if Gavin had actually stepped up and saved me from Daphne. Probably not. Myles shrugs.

"That's not laziness; that's ensuring his customers are entertained." I have to admit there was a lot of cheering when Daphne punched me, but at least somebody helped me escape the pub, too. Blood pouring down my face, I was helped out by a drunk who sadly was steadier on his feet than I was. Apparently, I'm not the first one Daphne has punched. It's been a while since she has broken anyone's nose though, and the other patrons seemed to appreciate the entertainment and the bonus of a broken nose. Someone even called for an extra round to celebrate, and that probably made Gavin and his cash register happy. "So, what are you going to do the day after tomorrow?" Myles asks.

"About what?"

"About the fact that Daphne and Claudia's parents are hosting their aunt's birthday." I consider saying I'm going to stay away, but I'm well aware I'm going, if Claudia will be there. That leaves only one option.

"Duck," I say and ignore Myles' roar of laughter.

CHAPTER 2

Hate

Daphne

Ryan. It's not his fault I hate him, honestly. Undeserved or not doesn't change a thing, and that doesn't mean I hate him any less, either. When he walked into the pub a few days ago I saw red and yet another reason for more drama with Claudia. If he doesn't already, this bastard is going to regret he *ever* came back here. I can't take any more drama. And that correlates perfectly with me punching him in a drunken fit of fury – or not. I think I might even have told him I hated him before I landed the first blow. I probably should have stopped drinking while I could still count the number of shots. And I probably should have stopped hitting him after the first blood spurted. Only I'm not smart like that, as my brother likes to point out far too often.

Claudia has been engaged three times to three different men within the last four years – not counting regular boyfriends in between – and Arthur is about to become the fourth. He has lasted for about a year, and compared to others, that's truly an accomplishment; maybe it's because they don't see each other that often. The church is already booked, but that doesn't necessarily mean a wedding is actually going to take place. The movie "Runaway Bride" could be inspired by the drama going on here, and it wouldn't be the first time Claudia cancels a wedding. Arthur has not even officially proposed, and if he is a smart man, then he'll wait and see if Claudia breaks it off with him *before* he spends money on a ring. I have little faith that will happen – I don't consider Arthur a smart man. And he'll be next on a rather extensive list of discarded boyfriends and broken engagements.

I wouldn't care much about the break-ups if it wasn't because each break-up has been drama like you won't believe. It's like Hollywood in the fifties, only the backdrop is not elaborate – it's provincial. Bloody Claudia. She should have gotten married and left town long ago, but I suppose it's not her fault she doesn't know all the elves have left Rivendell and gone to Grey Havens or got killed at Helms Deep. She's like a blond Arwen without a sword, a fast horse, or any kind of determination or courage. Meaning annoying and helpless like a damsel in distress from Medieval times. After twenty-five years I still don't understand how we can possibly be related. She doesn't understand either, and none one of us has ever been particularly happy about it.

If there's a man with a motorbike in a ten-mile radius wearing jeans and a leather jacket, that's the bed I'm heading for. If there's a boring man wearing a pastel knitted vest – preferably with stripes – that's where Claudia will be. And not anywhere near his bed. No, she'll torture him with family picnics and PG-13 outings and weddings, and if that doesn't scare him away … well, he asked for it then, didn't he?

The exception to all those boring pastel-dressed men was Ryan. He didn't wear vests – often – and he had an edge to him that none of the others had. He looks like the sort of man who could shag you in a dark corner at the aforementioned PG-13 wedding and then, with a straight face, go directly back to the party and dance with your grandmother. That edge and supposedly dirty mind were ultimately why Claudia decided he was not for her. He even expected them to be naked together at some point – imagine that! – and she found that notion completely ridiculous. Add to that, he was to be posted somewhere in Scandinavia for a year and even had the audacity to ask her to come with him and spend a whole year doing whatever she pleased.

She also thought he was too rebellious because he often wore jeans to family festivities. Too rough around the edges, too dangerous – or something like that. I almost threw up in my mouth each time she called Ryan a *bad boy* – she has no idea what that is – and at times like these, I'm somewhat thankful my family doesn't have a barn. I probably would have hanged myself.

Ironically the break-up with Ryan was the worst of them despite they weren't even engaged, and they only went out for about a month. Afterwards, there was constant – loud, crying, screaming, moaning – drama for weeks, and that is why I hate him so much. I'm forever traumatised – much like anyone present near the boxing ring when Rocky groans for Adrian or any neighbours when Stanley screams for

Stella. I swear I've had tics at the mere mention of the name Ryan ever since. Ryan Reynolds might be the only exception.

So, when I see Ryan with a black eye at my aunt's birthday two days after I punched him, I control my tics and snicker instead. I have absolutely *no* regrets. Even from a distance, I hate him. When he came back to town, he was pretty, and now he's not. Not quite, anyway. A broken nose and a black eye will usually do that for you. It's not surprising he's good-looking under the bruises and swelling, though – my sister has always had gorgeous boyfriends, and I suppose it's a plus having something pretty to look at while you're boring yourself to death. Arthur, the one she's set on marrying – at the moment, at least – is boring, too. And not quite as good-looking as Ryan.

Arthur wears striped knitted vests *often*. His pronunciation is too upper-class for the town, and it's something he does on purpose – like he belongs at court contrary to the rest of us – and that makes him a pitiful creature in my book. His family has a farm, he's an accountant and none of that merits any kind of upper-class if you ask me. He always says *do not* instead of *don't*. *It is* instead of *it's* and so on, like contractions are for illiterates or people who don't know any better. Looking at him right now, I think I might want to punch him even more than I did Ryan – and I'm even sober!

Claudia glides by me like she's floating or moving in slow motion – it's a particular talent of hers – and heads towards Arthur. We're far past Easter, but he looks almost like a dressed-up Easter Bunny with the pale yellow and light green striped knitted vest and furry hair sticking up at his neck. Some might say he'd fit right in with his new family. My mother loves pastels. My father is usually oblivious and doesn't even notice when my mother hands him a pastel lilac shirt to wear – I think it's a defence mechanism. My older brother Gary, who likes pastels too, considers himself an important man – he's not – and Claudia plays elf maiden most of the time, pastels included, of course. Families can be awkward, and ours is no exception.

Except for the time of year this is very much like the turkey curry buffet in "Bridget Jones' Diary" – my life is a bloody travesty, but at least I'm wearing my own clothes. Sadly, there's no Colin Firth to ease the pain, but ironically, my aunt's grey Pitbull is called Darcy, and at least he's roaming free among the guests. He's a sucker for attention, and since I'm not *that* fond of most of the people here, it suits me perfectly.

I'm on my knees on the kitchen floor. Darcy looks content and happy as only a dog can, and he looks like he's smiling. He's on his back, enjoying being petted, and I'm certain he'll follow me, begging for attention if I should ever *dare* stop. All four legs point straight up and he almost looks like a small table that's been turned upside down.

The swinging doors to the kitchen open, and I see Ryan enter. He flinches slightly when he sees me, but then he sighs and shakes his head. I hope it hurts.

"A Pitbull. Could you be any more cliché?" he scoffs. He considers me verily, and I don't blame him at all.

"A blue shirt. Could you look any more boring?"

"Absolutely," he says with a snort. "I could've worn a yellow, striped vest and tie like Arthur." I nod slightly because I'll give him that. Looking at Ryan, there's a vast difference between him and Arthur. Ryan has a beard in the making, a blue shirt, no tie, and a few buttons opened to reveal a few inches of what looks like a slightly tanned and not-too-hairy chest. He's also wearing dark jeans, and that makes him look … sigh … just perfect, honestly. If Arthur, on the other hand, ever decided to grow a beard, it would look like someone had rolled a woollen carpet over his head from his ass to his prick. I haven't seen it – his prick, that is – but I doubt he can be that hairy on his chest and neck only. Claudia appears happy with him – good for her since they're probably getting married and all – but I'd put him in line with the sheep at shearing time. Without a doubt, without regret. He'd probably shed enough hair to make a nice sweater.

Ryan edges into the kitchen, and he's smart enough to keep the kitchen counter between us. I might hate him, but I'd never just pounce on him while sober. Probably not. He opens the refrigerator and grabs a bottle of white wine. I pinch my eyes and glare at him, but he's smart enough to keep a safe distance too. I know I mostly got away with hitting him a few days ago because I surprised him. Ryan has no real reason to be afraid of me, and he's well aware. If he made even half an effort, I'm certain he could easily keep me at a safe distance, but that doesn't mean he's going to enjoy doing it. I understand why he finds that avoidance is a much better strategy. He's probably six-two, I'm barely five-two and nowhere near as strong as he appears to be. And speaking of … the boring blue shirt tightens around his bicep as he opens the wine, and my imagination even catches a glimpse of a tattoo beneath the fabric. He keeps his eyes trained on me while he opens the wine. Clearly, he doesn't want to be taken by surprise again. I might hate him, but I'll give him credit for not being entirely stupid – at least when it comes to this. His stupidity concerning my sister is another matter entirely.

He expertly opens the wine with a waiter's corkscrew, throws the cork into the bin, and puts the corkscrew back in its place. I suppose that's what comes from being raised by a mother who likes order and who primarily dresses in proper Chanel suits with matching jackets and skirts like she's the Jackie Kennedy of the village. She owns more wellies than anyone in town, matching the colours of her suits. She's the epitome of propriety and practicality and I'm certain she's been in the military at some point. Barking orders, making certain the privates had folded their underwear in a proper military manner before going home to raise her sons. Barking orders, making certain they knew how to fold their underwear and clean up after themselves.

My mother comes into the kitchen just as Ryan is leaving, and he smiles politely at her as he passes. My mother, on the other hand, looks strained, and she glances after him when he leaves.

"Oh, I'm so nervous," she says and wrings her hands anxiously. What else is new? But at least she acknowledges it this time without crying and too much fidgeting, and that's a definite win. "I just hope Ryan doesn't ruin anything."

"Ruin what?"

"Claudia's engagement, of course," she says almost desperately. My animosity towards Ryan is growing each second my mother seems worried. Lucky for him he just left the kitchen.

"Why would he do that?"

"Don't you remember the last time?" my mother asks, and I flinch at the memory. The experience has practically traumatised our entire family.

"It was her own fault," I insist. Ryan asked Claudia to come with him, but she wouldn't – despite it was only for a year and it's not like she had to give up any kind of work. When he left, she pretended she was some sort of heroine from a tragedy who wasn't given any choice and, therefore, lost her one true love.

"Could you just please make certain he doesn't stir up trouble?" my mother pleads. I hate it when she does that because I can't tell her no. Years ago, my mother had a nervous breakdown – I'm certain it was all Claudia's doing – and I'll do just about anything to prevent it from happening again. If Ryan makes her nervous … he's going down.

"How do I do that?"

"Don't let him anywhere near Claudia. Please, Daphne?" Contrary to Claudia, my mother is not hysterical and contrary to Claudia, my mother has had real difficulties, depression, and anxiety. Anxiety is no laughing matter, and I want to throttle Claudia each time she calls her own hysterics anxiety – it's not the same! The doctor agrees with me, but Claudia refuses to listen. She thinks she's entitled to spend hours at the doctor in order to make him see her way and grant her a diagnosis and pills. Like it's something to aspire to. I hate her when she does that. And so do the fifteen people in the waiting room who'll be delayed because she is determined the doctor *upgrades* her superficial hypochondriac sadness to depression. Sadness and depression are not the same, either! But Claudia refuses to acknowledge it. God, that pisses me off. Actually, there might be more people than Ryan and Arthur who deserve to be punched in the face.

"Can I hit him?" *Again.* I ask my mother.

"No, of course not." *Oops.*

"Then how do you suppose I make sure he does anything?"

"You know …"

"No, I don't. It's not like I have any chance of charming him," I protest. I'm pretty sure Ryan hates me as much as I hate him.

"You'll figure something out, I'm certain." She pats my hand encouragingly and then frantically hurries out of the kitchen. I don't want to have anything to do with Ryan. The only problem is I can't tell my mother no, and I'll protect her and her mental health until my dying breath – even if it means taking care of Ryan. Maybe even permanently. I should go look for the shovel I'm certain my father keeps out back. Too bad for Ryan.

CHAPTER 3

Pain

Ryan

Things are already looking up for me. I survived five minutes in the kitchen with Daphne, and the Riesling I've just opened is for Claudia. It's her favourite, and I'm heading straight for her with two glasses. I'm too preoccupied to notice Arthur until he's standing right in front of me.

"Hello, Ryan," Arthur says as I come to an abrupt halt, so I don't bump into him. "Ah, you brought the Riesling, perfect timing." Before I know it, he snatches the bottle and glasses from my hand, and unless I want to make a scene or spill wine all over, I have to let him keep it. It won't be appropriate to tackle him either, so I just grind my teeth as I watch him saunter towards Claudia, holding up the bottle like he's holding a trophy and like *he* was the one to win it. I wonder if he knows she doesn't like it when the wine has been sloshed around. She says it ruins the taste.

Since I'm not willing to make a scene, I'm left standing in the middle of the room, glaring at Arthur, who's fumbling with something in his pocket. They're getting married soon, and he hasn't officially proposed yet, so I have a rather good idea of why he's fidgeting. I'm just about to rethink my strategy about making a scene when someone claps my shoulder.

"Hello Ryan, welcome back." I turn and see Robert Collins. We went to school together, and even though we weren't friends as such, we got along fine.

"Thanks, Robert, how are you doing?" I ask as we shake hands.

"Better than you, it would seem," he says and nods his head slightly towards my face. "I look better, too," he says, grinning. And that's honestly a true tragedy. Of all the nice things you can say about Robert, not one of them is about how he looks. He looks like a blond pig who's learned to walk upright and dress himself. He's cross-eyed and has a large gap between his front teeth that always holds a *chunk* of food after he's been eating.

"Not that hard at the moment," I agree and silently *dis*agree.

"Not the welcome home present you'd hoped for, I take it?"

"Felt more like a surprise party gone awry." Robert chuckles, and I must admit, if I hadn't been the one on the receiving end of Daphne's anger, I would have laughed about it, too.

"She does that, you know? Surprise you."

"What are you talking about?"

"Daphne, of course. The whole town knows she's the one who hit you," he says happily, and I wouldn't put it past him if he'd been at the pub the other night, cheering loudly as Daphne demolished my face.

"Of course it does," I grumble.

"Don't worry," he says and claps my shoulder. "You're not the first. And at least you didn't hit her back."

"Has that ever happened?" I ask. Part of me completely understands how that would be tempting, and another part of me rebels. You *don't* hit women. Or children or animals, for that matter. You just *don't*. Despite there being no warm feelings between me and Daphne, and despite her being responsible for the soreness in most of my face, I can't even imagine what it would take to make me clench my fist and punch her face. Robert nods his head.

"Some wanker who thought he was king of the place because he's a distant Kensington relative."

"What happened?"

"Let's just say he got a lesson in dirty fighting."

"No shit," I grumble. I can well imagine Daphne fighting dirty. With her size, what else is she supposed to do when facing a man? Except *not* fight him – but that's not very likely, is it? Robert grins.

"Daphne got a black eye, and a tooth knocked loose, but that guy will probably be limping and have difficulties scratching his ass for the rest of his life whenever the weather turns cold. Not that we'll ever know because he's not welcome here anymore," he says ominously. I nod my head in understanding because that's another aspect of small-town mentality. We might not be thrilled about each other, but hell no, if any outsiders are allowed to make *any* kind of trouble.

"You ran him out of town?"

"Well, at least we took him to the emergency room when Daphne was through with him. But he didn't even come back for his fancy car."

"Never?" Robert shakes his head.

"Nah, we dragged it to Fernsby's field and removed the battery and fluids. The kids use it to play."

"It didn't run?"

"Bit difficult driving anywhere with four flat tyres."

"Four?"

"It happens," Robert says with a shrug before he wanders off. Yeah, sure, that happens. At least in this town, it does.

I look towards Claudia and Arthur, and he's finally stopped fidgeting. Daphne is right because you can tell he's Mr Boring just by looking at him. Nonetheless, he pulls out a ring and gets down on one knee. My gut clenches – this can't be happening! I might not have wanted to spill the wine and make a scene, but now I have to. I'm *not* tolerating that Claudia accepts Arthur's proposal.

I'm just about to say something – I have no idea what – when *a* ball smashes into *my* balls, bringing me to my knees with a thud and a groan. That overly happy creature of a Pitbull Daphne was petting earlier comes rushing, giving chase. Thankfully, the ball – the one the dog is chasing – has bounced off my groin and has rolled under the couch. Good luck with that, doggo, because that's the town's overweight vicar sitting there – and twenty-to-one he's not moving.

"Oh, so sorry," Daphne says smoothly. She's made her way to me, and somehow, I'm not surprised she is the culprit. She bats her eyes innocently, and I don't believe it for a minute. I'm still on my knees, gasping for breath through the pain when I hear a slightly hysterical squeal, and people are clapping. I know this means Claudia has just accepted a ridiculous proposal and I'm actually slightly impressed with Daphne's timing. She really nailed it – in more ways than one.

"You don't mean that," I croak as I slowly – and carefully – stand up despite the pain.

"That I might have stopped you from reproducing? You're right. I don't mean that at all."

"You bitch," I say and shake my head. If she had been a man, I would've punched him. Hard.

"You look good," she says with a saccharine smile that actually makes me shiver. When a hellhound bares its teeth at you, it's not necessarily a smile, you know? I look at her, and honestly, I don't know what to say. She's wearing a peasant blouse with embroidered flowers, a plunging neckline, and sleeves so wide it'll be a miracle if she doesn't clear the buffet in one sweep if she decides to eat anything. Underneath, she's wearing a short, red leather skirt so tight it looks like a second skin on her ass. She must be wearing the tiniest knickers on earth – *not* that I noticed it earlier when she was on her knees patting the dog, for any other reason besides I want to kick it. Her ass, that is, not the dog. I like dogs. I don't like Daphne. She's also wearing turquoise trainers, add her hair colour, and she looks very colourful, very much like a fucked-up rainbow.

"You look alternative," I sneer. She clasps her hand over her heart – cleavage – and sighs.

"Ryan, you say the sweetest things." She smiles, and for a moment, she almost looks like a woman. I'm not going to be fooled, though.

"Did you mean to mutilate me on purpose?"

"Maybe. Is it necessary?"

"What does that mean?"

"I'm not letting you ruin anything between Arthur and my sister."

"How could I?" I ask innocently.

"Oh please, you know how fickle Claudia is. Obviously." I grind my teeth because I don't need a reminder that all it took was five weeks of absence until my girlfriend declared she was engaged to another man. Technically, they were not engaged until a moment ago, but it still hurt. Five weeks. I mean, seriously, who does that? A teeny-weeny rational part of my brain doesn't understand why the rest of me is so eager for a repeat of that experience, but I don't seem to be able to help myself.

Daphne takes my arm and smiles as my mother approaches. She smells of flowers and something sweet I want to eat it along with strawberries on the buffet. Daphne, that is, not my mother. I squirm discreetly because nobody wants to make a scene when my mother is there – that is *not* tolerated. Daphne pinches my ass hard – and equally discreet.

"Smile, Ryan, or I'll tell your mum you were just about to object to the marriage," she whispers through clenched teeth. Somehow, Daphne knows that my mother doesn't think me being with Claudia is the most brilliant idea I've ever had, and I'm not dealing with both Daphne and my mother at once. I might be stupid once in a while, but basic survival instincts are not to be ignored. Even I know that. I'm not *that* stupid.

"Daphne, how wonderful to see you," my mother says happily. "I see you met Ryan?"

"Yes, we are just getting reacquainted," Daphne answers rather civilised. Reacquainted my ass – which incidentally is going to be sore tomorrow after she pinched me – because I've never really known Daphne. She has always been the younger and lesser sister. Ever seen Cinderella? Well, hello, ugly sister.

"I'm so happy Claudia is engaged," my mother says with a pointed look towards me. I manage a nod and a strangled smile – but only when Daphne pinches my ass hard again. If she keeps this up, I won't be able to sit down tomorrow. Bloody Daphne.

My mother doesn't think Claudia is a good match for me, and I'm certain she had a very large sherry to celebrate the day I left town – and unintentionally, Claudia. My mother was also the one who told Claudia that I was probably never *ever* coming back – and that I'd probably meet a wonderful *natural* blond Scandinavian beauty in Copenhagen, I would marry right away and start a family. I didn't, and there aren't *that* many. I did learn to ride a bike to work, though.

Besides the failed relationship with Claudia, it was a great year. Copenhagen is famous for urban planning and is among the most environmentally friendly cities in the world. There was much to learn, and not just about urban planning. Other colleagues were there to learn about resource and waste management and climate mitigation. The company language is English, and the Danes are pretty good at it in general, so I didn't learn much Danish. But along with my English colleagues, I often became the victim of an ancient Danish joke with foreigners: "rødgrød med fløde". Apparently, that never gets old. We continued to fail at the pronunciation completely, and the Danes continued laughing at us, but at least they paid for the beer.

As far as Claudia was concerned, I might as well have gone halfway across the world or to another planet. But the truth is, Copenhagen is not that far from here, and I could easily have come home for a weekend once I'd settled. But she could have come to Denmark, and she could have called too. She did neither. I was so angry and so disappointed. Every day, I hoped for a phone call from Claudia that never came. I hoped for an explanation that never came, either. When I heard about Claudia's "engagement" she had been engaged for a week. My mother deliberately didn't tell me anything and not so secretly rejoiced every day I didn't talk to Claudia.

That was then, this is now. I returned to town to get Claudia back. That hasn't changed – now I only have to break up an actual engagement in the process. But I'm not telling my mother until I've married Claudia – I'm not *that* stupid.

"Yes, we are, too," Daphne tells my mother and brings my attention back to the conversation. "We're all excited about Claudia starting a new life." Despite her pleasant smile, I sense an underlying tension in her statement.

"I understand perfectly well," my mother says kindly. Well, this is a strange experience … the Hellhound and the Colonel are talking amiably, and I'm standing here like I'm some sort of arm candy. I could've sworn my mother didn't like Claudia and her family at all. She casts the two of us a meaningful glance, which I don't quite understand, and then she smiles to Daphne and moves on. We both watch her carefully and only when she's engaged in a heated conversation about the town's name merely moments later do we let go of each other like we're both getting rid of something poisonous.

"Nice ass, Ryan," Daphne sneers and saunters away.

"Not anymore," I snap because she's practically mutilated it. Bloody Daphne.

CHAPTER 4

Fear

Ryan

Another day, another party. Today is the Kensington's silver anniversary. They're just as pompous as their name, and of course, their celebration is over the top, despite nobody truly believing they like each other that much anymore. They probably never did.

The celebration includes more than a hundred people. White linen tablecloths, place cards handwritten in calligraphy, and a luxurious tent with plenty of underpaid teenagers for waiters. Mrs Kensington declared they didn't wish for any presents but asked that money be donated to charity instead. Mr Kensington called that notion poppycock and declared he wished for large boxes of Cuban cigars and peace and bloody quiet to smoke them. Mrs Kensington declared he doesn't smoke and asked people to buy them chickens and goats in Africa. Mr Kensington then shouted he didn't bloody care about Africa and that he already had one farm animal. One he'd even married twenty-five years ago.

So, as far as a present goes, Myles and I did what every sensible adult man would do: left it to his mother. I have absolutely no idea what my mother came up with, and I honestly don't care. I'm here for Claudia, and I don't give a damn about goats, chickens, Cubans, or Africa.

The Kensington's anniversary is the biggest pretend party of the summer. It's not every year they make a public show of their arguing, but every year, the guest pretend they believe in their happiness. A lot of the summer events are ridiculous, but contrary to this one, others are often fun. A posh party in this town is equally misplaced and comical. Most here are *not* sophisticated people, but you've got to at least admire the effort people make when they dress up for the occasion. There are many too-tight, colourful polyester dresses here tonight and even a few strange hats that look like they were bought for a cheap derby day. I must admit I don't understand the whole hat thing. I went with Claudia last year, and she wore something that looked like a small clown's hat in yellow pastel and a veil that covered most of her face like a cobweb. You could hardly see her face, and she couldn't eat at all. Her drinks were served with a straw, and several times, I prevented her from bumping into tables and doors, and I even saved her from falling into the garden pond. I didn't understand at all why the hat was such a great idea, but I don't believe it was expected of me either. I just told her she looked beautiful, and apparently, that was all she needed.

I wonder if the Kensington relation that punched Daphne is going to be here. I seriously doubt it, but if he is, he deserves anything coming to him.

"The Kensington who punched Daphne, is he here?" I ask Myles.

"Only if he's suicidal," Myles scoffs and adjusts his cufflinks like he's going into battle.

"Do you know something I don't?" I ask.

"Plenty. Anything particular you're wondering about?" he scoffs arrogantly.

"About tonight."

"Watch your six."

"My what?"

"Your six." He looks at me and rolls his eyes like *I'm* the idiot here. Trust me, I'm not. "Your back," he elaborates, clearly irritated.

"You've been watching too many movies," I snort.

"Nonsense, it's a common expression."

"In *the military*, Drippy," I snap. "We're in Puddle-whatevertown, and you were never even a boy scout." He hates it when I bring that up because, contrary to him, I have been both a scout and later in the military. I think Myles spent those four years Googling military expressions from numerous different countries and practised sentences where he thought he could put them to good use. It didn't work, though, and I hardly understood what he was saying – it was complete gibberish.

"Well at least I know how to dress properly," he says and glances at my suit. There is *nothing* wrong with my suit, but Myles is wearing a tuxedo worthy of James Bond himself in an attempt to outshine everyone else. He hasn't said anything, but I suspect it might have something to do with the *maybe* appearance of the oldest Kensington daughter. Personally, I don't believe she'll be back in town until the last will and testament of *both* parents are to be read.

"With your luck, you'll probably be seated with the retirement home," I mock.

"As long as I don't sit next to Mrs Jeffries," Myles moans. A shiver runs up my spine, and I'm tempted to loosen my tie so I can breathe more easily. I'd forgotten all about her, but apparently, the old bat is still alive. She's a cougar of the worst kind – uninhibited, relentless, and decidedly unattractive.

"You always were a coward," I say and pretend I'm not terrified, too. He glances at me, and it's clear he doesn't believe my blasé attitude. Mrs Jeffries can put the fear of God into every male, and Mrs Jeffries … she likes her men young. Or at least considerably younger than she is, which really isn't that difficult to find.

I clap Myles on the shoulder and make my way towards the opening of the tent, where another underpaid teenager is standing. He's doing his best to look important and intimidating, and God help him, like an adult. As I approach him, I hold out a tenner, and his eyes are fixed on the money. I add one more, knowing how underpaid he is and knowing this will get me anything I want.

"Twenty if you change the seating," I say quietly. He glances at me, but his eyes keep flickering to the bills in my hand. "My name is Ryan," I tell him. "I want a seat next to Claudia, and I want Arthur seated far away from her." I added another tenner, and the teenager grabs them and quickly shuffles off with a quick nod. He returns from the tent only moments later.

"Table seventeen." I nod briefly and give him another tenner.

I struggle not to look too triumphant when we're finally asked to find our places for dinner. When I see Myles moping alone in a corner, it becomes almost impossible. I shouldn't be happy he's disappointed, but I am. Kensington's daughter is the worst snob this town has *ever* seen, and no one deserves to be saddled with her – not even Myles.

I stroll leisurely towards table seventeen and pretend I'm actually looking for a place card with my name on it. I greet the other guests at the table and sit. I can hardly wait for Claudia to sit down beside me. The chair next to me is pulled out, and I'm halfway out of my chair, turning my head in a panty-dropping smile when she sits down. And then my smile falls from my face faster than the snobbish Kensington daughter would drop an Android phone. Because it isn't Claudia who's sitting down next to me – it's Mrs Jeffries.

"Ryan," she says delightedly. She grabs my face with both hands and plants a sloppy pink lipstick kiss on my mouth before I have any time to object. I feel like I've just been licked on the mouth by a St. Bernard. It's disgusting, and I frantically wipe my mouth. A large blot of pink lipstick is smeared on the napkin, along with something that looks an awful lot like saliva. I almost retch. I instantly wave down a teenage servant and ask for a fresh napkin. He carries the old one away in two fingers like it's a biology experiment gone wrong. He's not entirely wrong about that.

Mrs Jeffries is a widow. Fifty-plus years ago, she was probably an attractive woman. Now she's over eighty, and too much sunbathing has caught up with her. She's no longer slim but bony and has saggy skin. She had her breasts done once, and now that she's become older, she looks like an internet joke. Everybody in town knows this because she always prances around wearing as little clothes as possible. A string bikini to a family outing or a cleavage to her navel. Tonight is, unfortunately, an excellent example. Her breasts look like someone has shoved a billiard ball into a pair of long, old football socks.

"Do you like my dress, Ryan?" she asks huskily and leans closer to me when she catches my *extremely* short glance at her cleavage. It's not because there's something nice to see. It's simply because it's so absurd you just can't help looking, just like you can't help yourself looking at something that's not supposed to be funny or something that's about to go wrong. "It's new," she discloses and leans even closer to me. I move as far away from her as I can without falling off my chair – I almost feel like I'm defying gravity – but she is not deterred and almost climbs onto my lap. She grabs my leg under the table, and I twitch in panic. Fortunately, it's my knee and not my thigh she grabbed, but my cock and balls are already looking for an escape and crawls towards my abdomen.

"I'm a Virgo," she says. "I'm *very* compatible with either Scorpio, Capricorn, Aries, Taurus, or Cancer. When's your birthday, Ryan?"

"July 26th."

"Close enough," she says and grabs my thigh hard. This is going to be the longest night in history. At least I'm sitting down, and Mrs Jeffries can't grab my ass. It's tender like hell after Daphne pinched me yesterday. I don't bruise easily, but I've got very noticeable blue marks. Bloody Daphne.

Dinner is horrible, to say the least. I hardly eat because I spend most of my time trying to fend Mrs Jeffries off. Despite my best efforts, she manages more slobby kisses – and unfortunately, each of them merits a clean napkin. I get a lot of pitying looks from just about every person in the room, but secretly, they're thrilled she's not their problem tonight. At least nobody's laughing at me – not even Myles – and if that's not a sign that I'm in real trouble, I don't know what is.

During dinner, I struggle to keep my manhood – in every sense of the word – and adulthood intact. I refuse to let Mrs Jeffries hand-feed me despite numerous attempts. I get a new napkin three times, and by the end of dinner, I'm in desperate need of a shower. Her perfume lingers in my suit because she's rubbing against me constantly. I can barely eat anything by myself because when she finally gives up trying to hand-feed me, she holds my arm so tightly I can't use the fork. No matter, because when she tells me she wants to give me a collar so I can be her favourite pet, I lose my appetite completely.

Particularly when she ensures me that the collar is everything I'll *ever* have to wear at her house and in her garden when I come to see her and offer up my *services*.

As soon as I make my escape from the table, I look for the teenager I paid to … well, absolutely nothing, as it turns out. When I see him standing by the opening of the tent, he flinches, and he even makes an attempt to escape before I get to him. He almost makes it when I grab him forcefully by the waistband of his trousers.

"What the hell happened?" I snarl as I pull him towards me.

"The woman in the green dress." The teenager glances over my shoulder. He looks absolutely terrified, and I know *exactly* who he's talking about even before I turn and see … Daphne … wearing an emerald green dress. The teenager is almost hyperventilating by now, and I release him and dismiss him with a nod of my head. I can't really blame him for being scared to death. Even wearing a dress, a hellhound is very recognisable.

As he scrambles away from me, I look at Daphne. Like many other women here tonight, she's wearing a hat, but contrary to most, I must grudgingly admit she doesn't look comical. It's a pillbox hat with a few feathers and a small veil, like she's just stepped out of a more sophisticated era. She's also wearing a wrap dress … and it wraps her all right. She's so much curvier than Claudia, with bigger tits and a rounder ass, and if she was human, she would be *extremely* attractive despite the ugly colours of her hair. Only she's *not* human. She's *not* an amazing-looking, fierce, sexy woman with the body of a bloody pin-up who should be painted on a fighter plane. Ironical since I know for a fact that she could put Memphis Belle out of commission faster and far more efficiently than the Germans did. She might look like either Peter Driben or Gil Elvgren made her up, but she's also the bane of my existence, the mutilator of my face and balls, and I hate her. Also, I might fear her more than I fear Mrs Jeffries. At least Mrs Jeffries is predictable, but you never can tell what Daphne is going to do or how much is going to hurt.

Like she can feel I'm staring at her, she turns toward me. She smiles at me devilishly and wiggles her fingers in a saucy wave from across the room. My cock and balls completely forget they've spent most of the night cowering in fear from Mrs Jeffries, and I have to remind them they're *not* looking at a human being right now, and they have absolutely no reason to feel enthusiastic about anything. Bloody Daphne.

CHAPTER 5

Panic

Ryan

I'm not giving up.

It's been three days since the disaster at Kensington's silver wedding day. But today is boating day with Mr Turner. My family – the Bancrofts – the Quintrells, and Claudia's family – the Fletchers, are going sailing. My mother probably had a large sherry for breakfast because – let's be honest – she's not that fond of spending time with Claudia's family. She's not that fond of Mr Turner either, and without question, this day is going to be quite the ordeal.

The sailing boat is monstrous and almost too big for the marina. Actually, I might not even be let on board if Mr Turner overheard that I called his toy a *boat* – because it's a yacht! Fifty-something feet of wasted money because he can neither tie a simple knot, tell port from starboard, or sail it himself, despite it contains every modern gadget you could ask for. The hired captain must earn most of his money on the indulgent smile he has plastered on his face constantly. Not only is the owner a helpless, self-important man, but he has also named the yacht The Princess. The official story is he named it after his late wife, but he really named it after his Shih Tzu. The dog has died too, and now he only has the yacht as a floating shrine to remind him of his lost love. The dog, that is.

If you are not used to sailing, there are a few things you should know: You *cannot* wear any footwear that doesn't have white soles because heaven forbid you should leave a dark footprint anywhere on the boat. It is simply *not* tolerated. You should also bring your own lifejacket unless you want to wear one that's not of this century and smells like it died a hundred years ago, too. Or even worse, you could wear one that's too small, and consequently, you'll be unmanned by a crotch strap that's too short. And most importantly: bring towels and clothes … lots and lots of clothes. Shorts for swimming, shorts for wearing, and some sort of hat or cap. A sweater, jeans, lots of socks, an extra towel, a waterproof jacket, and, of course, wellies and sunscreen. And preferably two of everything in case of rain, waves, wind, or sunshine. So, when I get to the marina, I'm carrying my own lifejacket and have a massive duffel bag on my shoulder. I've foregone the wellies simply because I can't stand the comments, I know my mother is going to make. The woman owns an ungodly number of fashionable wellies, but I only have one black pair. One which – according to her – makes me look like I'm either a drainage worker or a serial killer.

It looks like most of today's guests are gathered by the stern of the yacht, probably admiring the boat's ass by Mr Turner's request, but Claudia is standing alone, looking towards the sea. A light breeze is blowing, and her hair flows hypnotically in the wind – perfect. To get to her, I "only" have to sneak past my family and other guests, sidestep a pile of perfectly rolled up rope, and a woman standing slightly off to the side, looking like she's deliberately avoiding being associated with the yacht's worshippers. I understand her completely. She's wearing a dress and a black summer hat with a large brim, and she has a large, feminine bag on her shoulder. The dress is loose, and it flows in the wind, making the flower pattern look alive. I see the delicate bow at the halter neck, and a single ray of sun is caressing her flawless, naked back. Nice calves, gorgeous knees – she's probably someone from the Quintrell family I haven't met. As I get closer to her, I almost have to shake my head to clear it and keep my original destination in mind – Claudia. As I pass the woman, I smell something sweet that almost makes me want to lick her shoulder. It also causes some kind of déjà vu that confuses me. Why is that mouth-watering scent familiar?

I've almost made my way past her when she quickly turns around. Her massive shoulder bag hits my stomach with a forceful thud even Grond would envy. It almost feels deliberate. I have a feeling I'm balancing at the tip of my toes forever on the edge of the jetty like a cartoon character before gravity wins and pulls me into the water with an enormous splash. Being hit in the stomach makes me gasp for breath, and my mouth is immediately filled with dirty saltwater; I unfortunately swallow. I struggle to hold my breath, so I don't breathe in another mouthful. My clothes and the duffel bag immediately become heavy with water and pull me towards the bottom like an anchor being dropped. Not only that, but it feels like my body is going into shock because of the cold water. The British summer is mostly a joke, and it takes forever to heat up the sea to a decent temperature. Obviously, that hasn't happened yet. Head underwater, I panic and briefly wonder how long it takes for a human to drown as I desperately struggle to reach the surface. The life jacket is lying conveniently on the jetty where I dropped it.

"Oh, there he is," my mother says delighted when I finally get my head above water. Most guests are sending me dirty looks because falling into the water apparently made quite a splash. Myles is even shaking his stupid Panama straw hat to get rid of the water I've no doubt splashed all over it.

"For God's sake, Ryan," he complains.

"Ugh, I'm drenched," Claudia whines, and I look at her regretfully. Only I can't see more than a few specks on her dress, so why is she complaining? I seek out the attractive woman in the flowery dress who accidentally pushed me into the water. I almost swallow another litre of water when I see the woman is Daphne. Of course, it is. Who else? Now, I also see that the pattern on her dress is not flowers but skulls. Of course it is! And accident? The hell it was!

She looks like she was the one who got splashed the most, and it serves her right. Water is dripping from the brim of her hat, and the loose dress is sticking to her body like it's painted on. Contrary to others, she looks unconcerned, and though I'm loathed to admit it, she looks … the phrasing "wet dream" comes to mind. I don't want to think about that. I also don't want to consider I can still hear Claudia whining while Daphne looks at me with a satisfied smirk like she's struggling to hold back laughter.

"You're not supposed to swim in the harbour, Ryan," my father chides, but at least he bends and reaches for the heavy, drenched bag I'm struggling to free from my shoulder while I tread water. There's no way I can get out of the water with that thing over my shoulder. Finally, I give up and dip my head under the surface in order to lift the strap over my head and free myself.

"What on earth did you bring?" my mother asks as my father uses considerable strength to drag the wet duffel bag onto the jetty. I don't answer her because I brought less than half the things, she no doubt forced my father to pack. I haul myself out of the water. I was not in there that long, but my teeth start clattering when a gust of wind sweeps through the marina. I'm absolutely drenched, and my suede trainers – with the white soles, of course – will probably never be the same again.

"Ryan, you can't go sailing like that." Mr Turner looks at me as I stand sogging wet on the jetty. The puddle at my feet is growing fast and spreading towards the other guests. Most are wearing wellies – they retreat – but Daphne is wearing orange ballet flats. Of course, she is. And she's not moving a single inch from the growing puddle either. Of course, she isn't. "The boat will get wet," a very concerned Mr Turner says with a disgusted frown on his face. I catch a glimpse of Daphne pinching her lips at the irony and I'm certain she just barely managed to spare Mr Turner a snarky remark. Despite it all, I'm having difficulties keeping a straight face, too.

"Well, we can't have that," Claudia chimes in supportively, and Mr Turner sends her a polite smile, seemingly grateful that at least one person understands his concern about getting his boat wet. Daphne rolls her eyes under the brim of the summer hat at the stupidity, and it's so strange that she, of all people, is the one I'm in accord with. There's no doubt my mother finds it equally stupid, but her main priority is to keep me away from Claudia, even if it means agreeing with Mr Turner. Apparently, that is how far we've come.

I'm left behind, and I can only stand there and watch as the other guests get on board and the smiling captain manoeuvres the *boat* away from the jetty. Daphne, that bloody bitch, is smiling at me from the stern. I'm so bloody cold my teeth are chattering, and my body is shivering. There's not a single ray of sunlight anywhere near this part of the marina. Of course, there isn't.

I pat my wet clothes, looking for the important things which aren't there. Discouraged, I look at the water, and I'm certain I see the important things – keys, phone, wallet – glinting dimly from the bottom. Bloody Daphne! The marina's water is dirty, and I now smell like diesel, and God knows what. A dead duck floats along with rubbish and seaweed. A swan is cruising ominously toward me like it's pretending it's a great white shark and not a great white bird. Right now, I don't care because I'm certain it can't be as bad as Daphne. Nothing can.

The harbour master comes running just as I'm about to jump in.

"You're not allowed to bathe in the harbour," he shouts, and I perform another cartoon-like balance act on the edge of the jetty, but at least I manage to stay above water this time.

"My keys and phone are at the bottom," I tell him.

"Why?

"I fell into the water." He looks at me funny, and then he glances around. The jetty is wide enough for an elephant, so I can't really say I blame him for wondering what the hell I've been doing, particularly since I'm now the only person there.

"How on earth did you manage that?"

"Because that bloody woman is the devil," I say agitated, pointing toward The Princess. "She's a saboteur and a danger to everyone around her. She's a bloody hellhound in disguise, a noisy bitch, and the bane of my existence. She breaks bones and balls and smashes faces," I say angrily and point to my nose, whose bandage, by the way, is floating somewhere in the water. The harbour master almost looks impressed by my outburst. "Not to mention she seated me next to Mrs Jeffries."

"That's bloody bad luck," he says, absolutely horrified. No, it wasn't bad luck. Merely Daphne.

"You don't say?"

"Well, I suppose you can go in then. Wouldn't recommend it, though. The water is a bit cold. Quite dirty, too." I just glare at him because, believe me, I know.

I look up just in time to see The Princess glide out of the marina. It looks like the sun is shining out at sea. Claudia and the rest of the guests are nowhere to be seen, but Daphne with her stupid summer hat is still standing at the stern. She gives me a queenly wave, and from a distance, she almost looks classy enough to belong on a yacht. Bloody Daphne.

Patience

Ryan

The least prestigious and most hated event in the summer is the seniors' market day. On this day people in town are more or less forced to acknowledge they have an older family member. Most families are quite happy they can ignore them for the remainder of the year. They only dust them off in the summer and allow them to participate in festivities where families can pretend the old person roaming free, wearing only a diaper and a sixpence is none of their concern.

While most families can survive being at the same event as their older relatives, most can't bear the thought of participating today. It's the only thing happening, and it's considered bad form to plan something that overlaps with the seniors' market. But still, nobody wants to be there. It's the day when most people take a break from socialising and eating. Today they mow the lawn, water plants, or recover after too many parties. They'd rather do the dishes than attend the seniors' market for more than ten minutes and make their relatives happy. The clever parents even drop off their children, telling them they'll have such a wonderful day with their grandparents before they themselves escape to their home.

Most of the seniors require patience none of us possess, particularly since all they really want is to discuss the name of the town. I couldn't care less what they call this bloody place. I don't even want to be here! Myles hates it too; only he's ruthless enough to innocently enquire about whatever happened to the "Mudpuddletown" name whenever someone approaches him. Nobody wants to answer *that* question, and he's very quickly excused from the conversation. He's quite clever sometimes.

My family doesn't have any older relatives participating in senior's market day, but my mother makes us go anyway and forces us to stay for at least an hour. The way she sees it, it's good form, and besides, Myles and I won't have the choice of *not* going when it's her and my father living at the local retirement home, so we might as well get used to it. So, just like when we were children, Myles and I were shoved into my parents' Vauxhall this morning. My mother doesn't trust either one of us to show up at senior's market day if we're left to our own devices. She's probably right not to. She's quite clever too sometimes.

The senior's market day is held on the outskirts of town. I've got to admire their way of thinking because they've set up their market day on the field because it's next to the largest road near town. They do this, hoping strangers will happen upon their market and delight in buying local handiwork that costs a fortune. It's an excellent idea, only the largest road is not that large, but most of all I'm certain even from a distance people can see how horrible everything is. I'm wearing my wellies because anything else would be stupid, considering we're in a muddy town and on top of that going to a field. My black wellies elicited the usual frown from my mother, and Myles whispered, "I know what you did last summer," in an ominous voice.

Mr Dawson once held the record for the tallest man in town. Since old age has caught up with him, he's shrunk an inch, if not two, but he's still taller than me. He usually wears red braces that pull his trousers so high I can't help but think it must be very uncomfortable. That also leaves his trousers even shorter than they have to be, but it's clear he's made an effort to look nice. He's a thin man, and the children in town call him Stick Man. I think he looks more like Jack Skellington – he's equally pale, has large, dark eyes and no hair. He used to work for the town's waterwork and was devastated when they told him it was time to retire. Since then, he's been taken on any kind of project he could, and today looks like it's no exception. When I arrive with my family, it's no surprise he's the first person I see, standing near the muddy car park in his wellies, holding a clipboard.

My parents and Myles say hello to Mr Dawson, but when he sees me, he grabs my hands with both of his like he's happy and exceedingly grateful to see me. I have absolutely no idea why my presence should merit that kind of reaction. I hardly know the man.

"Ryan, I'm so happy you agreed to help."

"I did?" I ask because this is the first I've heard about it. Mr Dawson shows me the clipboard that holds an extensive, and impressive schedule.

"Now, I have you at the knitting booth at ten for an hour. The basket shop for an hour and a half. The pottery booth for another hour – I'm certain they'll bring you a sandwich for lunch, at least I hope they will – and arts and crafts will need you at one thirty sharp for an hour. Then it's the knitting booth again for an hour. Painting booth follows until I can get someone to relieve you." He pauses after that very impressive and utterly horrible narrative about how my day is going to transpire. He smiles gratefully and puts a frail hand on my shoulder. "I'm very grateful you are here, Ryan. We couldn't do this without you."

"But …"

"I've made a copy for you, of course," he says over my objection and hands me an entire stack of handwritten papers. "I've also added descriptive notes and contact information. Here, I'll show you where the knitting booth is." Confused and numb, I follow him across the field. I attempt to ask him about the volunteering part, but he rambles on about the change in a cigar box and how he's glad I'm wearing wellies because the painting booth is set up in a rather large puddle. When I get there, I should take care not to step on the duck that refuses to leave, and I should just ignore it if it pecks me.

At the knitting booth, I'm surrounded by at least ten old ladies. They chatter like the market day is the second coming, and like I'm Christ himself, they're that grateful. Mrs Allen even grabs my hand and squeezes it gently with arthritic fingers.

"I'm very grateful, Ryan. I don't know how I would manage an entire day in the booth." And that's when my conscience kicks in. God, I'm stupid.

"You're welcome," I say gently. I don't think I manage a proper smile, but I must look friendly enough for her to hug me.

"My daughter should've been here to help me, but something came up," she says when she pulls away from me. She raises her chin, but I see her eyes are watering slightly. She probably knows absolutely nothing came up – at least nothing important – and she's trying to pretend she's not disappointed and hurt at all. Whether it's for her own benefit or mine, I don't know. I don't question it either, but I truly appreciate it.

"Well, that happens," I say politely.

"I suppose." She doesn't believe me, and I don't blame her at all. Besides, we both know the truth. I glance around the knitting booth, and I just know this is going to be the longest hour of my entire life.

After about half an hour, I see my parents coming my way, dragging Myles behind them like a tired puppy that has decided it doesn't want to walk anymore. My mother looks rather pissed, but I suppose it's because she lost me rather quickly when we arrived at the field, and she probably thinks I made a quick escape. If only … When she glances at the knitting booth, her anger turns to surprise when she sees me among miscellaneous knitted horrors.

"Ryan, what on earth are you doing?" she asks baffled.

"Volunteered, it would seem," I say drily. I have a sneaking suspicion Daphne is behind this. Not even Myles is this evil.

"That's awfully nice of you, dear." She looks perplexed and rather worried like she's considering if I've lost my mind. Both Myles and my father look like they've just discovered an elephant in the front garden and are thinking, "That's not supposed to be there." I wholeheartedly agree.

"How long are you in for?" Myles asks like we're talking about prison. He's not completely wrong about that – it certainly feels that way already.

"All day, apparently." Myles looks horrified and confirms my assumption he had nothing to do with this, because he's not that good of an actor. If he truly had something to do with this, he'd look far more gleeful.

"Suppose you can catch a lift back with Mr Dawson?" my father asks. He hates the seniors' market day as much as everyone else, and he's making sure he doesn't have to return here later. I just nod because there's no reason to include my family in my sufferings – not even Myles, considering he had nothing to do with this. I definitely suspect someone else. Someone far more diabolical. Bloody Daphne.

Most people who turn up here today are merely paying a duty visit, and they don't stay long. My family is no exception, and they leave after an hour. They've stayed longer than most, and that's rather sad, considering we don't even have relatives here. The only people who are here all day are the seniors, the children who have been dumped by their parents, me, and apparently Daphne. As probably the only person in town, she doesn't seem to own wellies. Today, she wears trainers that look like they were red this morning but now appear mostly muddy brown. They must be soaked, which just proves how utterly stupid she is, considering we're spending the entire day on a field.

I spend the day manning different booths in an in vain attempt to sell some of the paintings and knitted dogs the seniors have made during the winter workshops. I don't have much luck, but I buy two knitted animals myself. One for my mother and one for Myles – simply because I hate him, and this mousy thingy looks like it's been made by a blind person. It's actually rather scary.

There are not that many visitors and the seniors' attempt to contribute to the town's summer festivities with their market day is mostly ignored. And it's not because of the distance to the field. People have no problem driving more than thirty miles to go sailing, so three miles to a field isn't far. Unless it's for the senior's market, apparently. I'm not going to admit to Daphne that, somehow, being here today almost makes me feel like a decent human being. She's not going to get credit for that because she doesn't deserve credit for anything nice. But if it wasn't for her, I'd have done like everyone else – stayed away.

At three-forty-five, I catch a glimpse of Claudia arriving. I see her leave before four o'clock. At five-thirty, I'm still here. Bloody Daphne.

At least Daphne has the decency to stay the whole day as well. She's not enrolled herself in the booth manning schedule like I apparently have, but she's been mingling all day. I think she's been trying to entertain the seniors and attempting to keep their spirits up despite the neglect from their families. I've heard her most of the day because she's an awfully primitive creature who talks too loudly and laughs even louder. She has no problem taking off her shoes and running barefoot in the mud to play with the children who have been dumped here by their parents. A red-haired boy who's missing one of his front teeth even declares loudly it's the *best* day of summer just after Daphne has caught him in a game of tig. She hasn't thrown any mud at me yet, but mud has never bothered anyone here, so maybe she just considers it a wasted effort.

For once, the seniors haven't discussed the town name; they've been busy watching their grandchildren play and have fun. Despite the cold tea and the horrible sandwiches, everybody seems to agree with the boy: this is the best day of summer. I, on the other hand, am not entirely convinced.

While Mr Dawson was once the tallest man, Mrs Cross is the smallest woman in town. She is four-seven, and her entire appearance is fragile. She could easily fit into the chequered trolley she brings to the supermarket. I'm certain she buys her clothes in the children's section, and that is confirmed when I see her wearing a Pokémon T-shirt with an amount of glitter no adult would wear if they had any other choice.

Everyone knows Mrs Cross, and unfortunately, everyone knows her nephew Neil, too. He's a large, stocky man with an unhealthy-looking rosy complexion that comes from drinking too much. He's also very loud and very stupid, and it's no secret he's in a bit of a fix because he owes money to a few bookies. Something about horses. It's also no secret he's waiting for Mrs Cross to either die so he can inherit or give him money while she's still alive – whatever comes first. He doesn't care much either way. When a hush falls over the crowd of seniors sitting by the picnic tables, I immediately know something is wrong. And sure enough, I hear a loud, angry voice:

"Just pay up, you dirty, old bag." What the hell? I'm certain I break the seniors' booth protocol as I leap over the table with painted horrors – yes, it is possible wearing "I still know what you did last summer wellies" – and head for the area with the picnic tables. But someone has made it there before me. I hear Daphne's voice loud and clear – and pissed.

"Let go of her, Neil!" As I get there, I see Daphne facing off with Neil. He has grabbed Mrs Cross by the arm, and the tiny woman looks even smaller than usual standing there next to the monstrosity that is her nephew. Daphne doesn't look much bigger, and I feel an equal pinch of dread, admiration, and annoyance. How can she be so bloody stupid?

"Stay out of this, Daphne," Neil says with a growl that would make any ogre jealous.

"Go fly a kite, Neil!" she yells. "Let go of her, or you'll be sorry."

"Who's going to make me?"

"Who do you think?" She advances towards Neil, and I feel a twitch of panic. I might hate Daphne, but I'm not going to stand passive and watch as a large man attacks a much smaller woman.

"I think you should leave now," I say and channel the voice of Cole, my superior in the military, as I quickly make my way toward Neil. My hands are fisted, and I'm almost looking forward to this. I can't punch Daphne, but by God, I can punch Neil. He spins around to face me, and that's all the distraction Daphne needs to stab his hand with a fork. A fork. I'm only surprised she hasn't brought her own pitchfork from hell. If the situation wasn't so tense, I might have laughed at the absurdity and stupidity of the situation. Nonetheless, Neil releases his aunt with a yelp, and Daphne hauls Mrs Cross behind her for protection. Blood is pouring from Neil's hand as he yanks the fork out, and he absently puts his hand to his mouth. With the stench of liquor coming from him, I'm certain he just sterilised the wound as well.

"Such a pretty face," he slurs as he looks at me. "Who punched you?"

"Someone with far bigger stones than you," I snap. I'm not lying because no matter what I think of Daphne, she's definitely got balls. She's impulsive, too, and consequently stupid.

"Go get him, Ryan," an old woman shouts, and several seniors chime in encouragingly. I have no doubt they despise Neil. I also have no doubt they're mostly looking for something to entertain them. And if Neil knocks me out, they're probably counting on Daphne to either scare him off or finish him somehow. She'll probably do it too.

Neil charges me with a roar, and he almost makes it too easy for me. I sidestep him, trip him, and kick his ass hard, sending him sprawling into a puddle. Of course, there's a puddle. Two ducks quack loudly and unhappily as they're chased from their residence by the three-hundred-pound lump of a human being. He sputters and swears, and a mousy voice from the flock of seniors shouts:

"No profanity!" I don't think Neil cares as he staggers to his feet. The puddle and ground are red with blood – so typical for Daphne to turn an ordinary steak fork into a potential murder weapon. Neil's hand is bleeding profusely, and I feel a surge of satisfaction knowing I'm not the only man Daphne has made bleed recently. As soon as he gets on his feet, I grab his collar.

"Get the fuck out of here, Neil. Man up. Make your own bloody money and stop harassing your aunt." I push him forcefully away from me. He staggers but manages to stay on his feet, and then he wobbles towards the car park, mumbling something nobody can hear. Nonetheless, one of the seniors shouts:

"No profanity!" And then the flock of seniors starts talking all at once.

"Is he driving like that?"

"I've already called Morris."

"He shouldn't be driving."

"Thank you, Ryan."

"Don't thank him. He ruined the entertainment, didn't he?"

"Morris will stop Neil."

"Morris is drunk, too."

"He's allowed to be drunk. He *is* the police."

"Gavin should stop serving him."

"It's his father."

"Has anyone seen my teeth?"

"That was very brave of you, Ryan."

"Did Morris pick up the phone?"

"Yes, he did."

"Thank you, Daphne." That's Mrs Cross. Most of the other voices just blend together, and it sounds like I'm standing in a barn full of chickens. I can't tell them apart, and they're also making about as much sense as a flock of chickens: absolutely none at all.

While they all seem grateful, none of them consider releasing me from my booth duties, and I get to stay to the bitter end. Parents have been here to pick up their children – sort of. If sitting in your car, honking and texting is considered picking up. Most children hug Daphne goodbye, and the red-haired boy looks slightly teary when he asks Daphne to be his aunt.

"Of course I will, Alex," she assures him as she hugs him tight. His head reaches just under her tits, and when he pulls away from her, he has a delighted smile on his face, and I can honestly say I don't blame him. I still feel a pinch of annoyance. Clever little prick, isn't he?

I help pack up everything the seniors have brought to the field. It's difficult to accept they brought it all here without a lorry because the amount of … junk … is unbelievable. They stack, squeeze, and jam everything together and secure it partly with ropes. I have a sneaking suspicion that if Neil hadn't shown up and made trouble, Morris would have received a prank call drawing him away from town, so he wouldn't be here to see this. Morris might be drunk and not very clever, but even he would probably react to the absurd parade of overloaded cars. I feel like I'm in the middle of either a meme or a Guiness World Record attempt.

At the retirement home I have to wait for Mr Dawson to get out of the car. I have to wait for him to remove numerous boxes, a stack of knitted sweaters – at least that's what I think it is – a teapot from between my knees, and a few embroidered pillows from between my feet before I have any chance of getting out of the car. There's a quacking sound somewhere in the back, and I think we might unintentionally have brought a duck home with us.

I help him unpack the trailer. The folding chairs and tables go into the shed, and a considerable pile of handcrafted horrors that haven't been sold go into the common room. I keep an eye out for falling objects, but I also keep an eye on Daphne. I'm keeping her within my line of sight because I'm not going to be surprised by her again. God only knows what she'll come up with. She looks at me from the corner of her eye, and a small and decidedly evil smile spreads on those suck-worthy lips. I have no doubt she knows she's unnerved me.

"So nice of you to stay and help out the *entire* day, Ryan," she says loud enough for even the deaf seniors to hear. She sends me a satisfied smile and any lingering doubt I might have had disappears. I have absolutely no doubt at all she's the one who volunteered me. Bloody Daphne.

CHAPTER 7

Anger

Daphne

Ryan is angry. Actually, that might be an understatement. Ryan is furious. When he enters the pub later that evening, everyone takes one look at him and then gives him a wide berth. I avoid him too for as long as I can considering I'm at work, mostly because he makes me want to fan myself. Angry Ryan is *seriously* hot. Unlike most of Claudia's ex-boyfriends/ex-fiancées/ex-whatevers, Ryan has something rough hidden beneath that polite exterior. How the two of them ever ended up together is a true mystery. He definitely proved that roughness at the senior's market earlier today. Watching those large hands clench into fists made *certain parts* down below clench in me, too. Amidst the chaos I was practically drooling. Claudia would have fainted – dramatically, of course.

I know my sister is pretty to look at, but she's also completely oblivious to anyone and anything but herself. She has also proudly told me that she hasn't had sex since she was eighteen. Two questions – at least – are begging to be answered. One: How the hell did she keep her hands off Ryan? And two: Does she even know how hairy Arthur must be?! If not, then she's in for one hell of a surprise if they actually end up getting married. Nonetheless, she has managed several engagements and boyfriends, and it would seem my sister has successfully rewritten "Why buy the cow when you can get the milk for free?" to "If you don't buy the cow, you don't get any milk at all. Not even a single drop". I wonder if that only happens in small towns with a dairy production.

"Hey Ryan, what can I get you?" I ask politely as he comes to stand by the bar. He looks at me. He keeps looking at me, and for every moment that passes he looks more and more angry. I force myself to keep standing in front of him. I feel somewhat safer knowing there's a counter between us. Unless he's some kind of ninja, he won't be able to reach me easily. If he actually goes for it, I'm not going to get any help from either Gavin or the patrons. They'll probably start placing bets on the outcome.

"I don't hit women," he says slowly, like he's about to reconsider.

"Neither do I," I say honestly. I slap my hands on my cheeks and open my mouth in a dramatic gasp like I've seen Claudia do about a hundred times. "Oh my God, you're saying I shouldn't have hit you?" He clenches that all too-masculine jaw, and he's obviously struggling to remain calm.

"You broke my bloody nose, Daphne," he shouts angrily.

"Uhm, oops?" I say with a shrug. I actually feel a bit guilty about that. I was in a sodding bad mood that night, and seeing him made my temper get the best of me. I'm not admitting anything, though.

"Have you been to prison?" he asks me. "Seriously. Have you practised your punch on other inmates?"

"Did you go to an all-girls school to practice your wining?" I snap and forget all about feeling guilty.

"You are a bloody bitch."

"So, you think I should apologise?"

"For breaking my nose, smashing my face, *or* my balls?" I lower my gaze to his groin, and damn, that *does* look like a nice package.

"Looks like it's all still there," I say with a smirk. Ryan doesn't return my smile at all; he looks like he's grinding his molars to dust. "They must be healed by now," I add with a shrug and pretend the damage I've done to him so far is trivial.

"You pushed me in the marina, and you succeeded in drowning my phone."

"That's what insurance companies are for," I say nonchalantly.

"Mrs Jeffries," he shouts.

"Definitely insurance company," I say drily.

"They don't cover a cougar attack."

"Then a restraining order."

"The seniors' market."

"Your place in heaven is secured."

"At least that's something – you won't be there," he growls, and then he stalks off. I swear I can almost see steam coming out of his ears.

"If you don't want to see me, then why come in here?" I yell after him. But I know why. Gavin's pub is the only one in town, and unless you want to drink and drive, you have nowhere else to go. Too bad for Ryan.

*

The next day might be the worst day of summer because it's the Pink Party. This is probably the stupidest event of them all because it basically started out as a celebration for a vegetable – the beetroot. Then everyone found out how awful a meal consisting entirely of beetroot actually was and local geniuses – I use the term lightly – came up with the Pink Party instead.

Mr and Mrs Graham are the "genius" couple hosting The Pink Party and they're also some of my parent's closest friends, so there's no sitting this one out. They have no birthdays during the summer, no anniversaries, and everyone thought it was improper to celebrate the death of Mr Graham's mother. Mrs Graham thought it was a marvellous idea. They got a goldfish one year, but no one here cares about celebrating a goldfish. If the town is going to celebrate any kind of pet, it has to be at least the size of a cat. Unfortunately, Mr Graham is allergic to just about everything with fur – that might even include Arthur – and he quickly found out the town is not about to participate in celebrating a hairless cat. So, that is why they decided to claim the Pink Party as theirs to at least get some kind of attention. They hide the hairless cat somewhere upstairs.

Every year, the Grahams struggle to make it a super fun challenge to come up with all sorts of exciting, pink-coloured dishes. Nobody thinks it's fun, nobody thinks it's exciting. I cracked the code for a successful Pink Party last year: I eat an awful lot of salmon and drink plenty of rosé and don't really care about the rest. The men eat ham. Lots and lots of ham. The children eat macaroons and pink pasta. Someone has made a pink pie, someone has made devilled eggs and judging by the looks of it, the devil definitely had a hand in this – they look horrible.

At The Pink Party, you must be dressed primarily in pink – another "genius" idea by the Grahams – and all of the food must be some shade of pink, too. The men in town have argued that a steak is mostly pink before it's grilled, but it was not allowed. It wasn't pink enough – because it's always grilled to ashes and would ruin the look of the buffet. But when Ryan arrives is when I decide there's definitely meat at this party after all.

The best part of the day is the arrival of a group from the retirement home wearing Pink Ladies jackets, Grease-style. But the award for classiest outfit goes to Ryan without question. He's wearing a pair of burgundy-coloured jeans and a light pink dress shirt. Contrary to other men, he doesn't seem uncomfortable wearing anything besides grey or navy blue. It's almost going to be a shame ruining it.

The kitchen table serves as a buffet, and most of the food is unidentifiable. I swear some of the food just looks like it's been spray-painted pink. I know my mother has made some kind of beetroot salad. It's in a large glass bowl on the counter, and I have a clear view of the beetroot juice and dressing at the bottom. There's quite a lot, and it suits my purpose perfectly.

I know Ryan and Myles' mother has made macaroons, I know Ryan is tasked with bringing them to the buffet, and I know Ryan is about to regret it. The basket holding the macaroons is rather cute. Pink macaroons, pink napkins, and a bow, of course. Ryan looks almost comical carrying it around, and I snap a picture of him – I don't quite know why I can't help myself. But if there ever was a man able to carry a handbag or a pink basket with a bow and still preserve the tiniest hint of masculinity, it would probably be him.

Claudia is in the kitchen, too. She probably got lost because there's no chance, she's here to help my mother set everything up. Quite the contrary, she's claiming she's gotten something in her eye and demands my mother's *complete* attention when she demands my mother looks at it. That my mother has something more important to do doesn't deter her at all.

When Ryan enters the kitchen, I carefully take the large bowl of my mother's beetroot salad from the table. His eyes are fixed on Claudia, and he doesn't notice anything else. He absently puts the basket on the table next to a strange-looking pasta dish, and I quietly move to stand behind him. When he turns, he bumps into me and, more importantly, bumps into the large glass bowl. It tilts – with my help – and he's immediately drenched as beetroot salad pours over him. He looks like he's just about to apologise – at least until he notices it's me standing in front of him. His face then turns into a threatening scowl and it's clear he's definitely still angry. I make sure to discreetly tip the heavy bowl to pour all the dressing from the bottom over him. His jaw clenches, he pinches his eyes for a brief moment before he opens them and looks down. He looks like he's barely keeping himself from strangling me. I suddenly feel like it would've been a good idea to bring the shovel I saw not far from the front door inside with me.

"Oh," my mother exclaims loudly and comes rushing. She's probably just saved my life because Ryan looks like he's about to explode. It's only fair my mother saves me – it's her ploy, after all. "Now, don't you move, Ryan," she says frantically. "We can't have beetroot all over the kitchen floor. It will stain."

"Oops," I say because I'm *not* going to apologise. My mother starts tearing off sleeves of kitchen roll and hands it to me. She's probably hoping I'll accidentally punch him, too – despite she's told me I couldn't.

"You'll probably want to *walk* all the way home and get changed," she tells Ryan. "You can't risk ruining the interior of our car. It will stain." I pat his stomach hard with the kitchen roll, but surprisingly, he doesn't huff, and that only makes me pat it harder.

"Mother?" Claudia whines. Ryan keeps ignoring me as my mother rambles on.

"It's a new brand. Three plies," my mother discloses frantically about the kitchen roll like she's in sales. I don't think Ryan appreciates that at all right now – even though he should. I absently pat the hard stomach to dry him – well, actually, I'm doing my best to make the wet shirt stick to his abs so I can see them. They feel divine. I'm also seriously considering going to my knees in front of him to … wipe the floor, of course.

"What's this?" Claudia asks. She has finally given up getting my mother's attention from afar and is approaching the mess surrounding Ryan.

"Ryan had a small accident," my mother says smoothly, like she's talking about a toddler who's just pissed his trousers. Ryan scowls at me, and there's no doubt in my mind that my mother's degrading comment isn't making anything better for me at all. I wonder how far I'll get if I make a run for it. As long as I make it to the shovel by the front door, I should be okay. Maybe I should just whack him with it and get it over with. Afterwards, I can use the shovel to dig a hole for his body. Come to think of it, it's perfect.

"I detest beetroot," Claudia says with disgust clear on her face, making Ryan look queasy. But only for a moment before he glares at me. He silently mouths *bitch* to me while my mother is turned towards a dramatically faint-looking Claudia. I'm only surprised Ryan didn't slice the finger over his throat because he truly looks like he's about to kill me.

Claudia thinks beetroot smells and it reminds her of blood. I'm certain she only managed to stay in the kitchen this long because that's where my mother was. If Claudia had to command *all* of her attention, she had to be here too. I suspect my mother deliberately surrounded herself with beetroot in a vain attempt to escape her. Only she underestimated Claudia's need to be the centre of her attention. Still, if my parents were smart, they'd start eating beetroot every day to get Claudia out of the house.

If Claudia had seen how much blood Ryan's nose and eyebrow drew when they cracked, she'd probably have performed a Sleeping Beauty and pretended to sleep for a hundred years. Actually, that is not the worst scenario I can think of. I find myself considering how to make Ryan bleed again.

"You did that on purpose," Ryan snarls when he looks at me.

"Now Ryan, that's not nice," my mother chides. She sends him a look I've seen a thousand times when I got scolded as a child. My mother hasn't always been so feeble, and thankfully, she's momentarily found some backbone to protect me while I'm doing her dirty work. He sends her an apologetical look and gives her a small smile.

"I'm sorry, Gemma," he says politely. "I'm certain it was an *accident*." He grinds out the word, almost like it's causing him physical pain. His clothes are completely ruined, but the way I see it, he's just lucky we're nowhere near the outdoor fireplace – because then I might've been tempted to set him on fire.

"Very unfortunate," my mother says empathetically and nods her head gravely. "Please don't be angry. I understand how it can seem like Daphne doesn't like you at all. Truth is, Daphne has always been slightly clumsy." That's an obvious lie and the whole town knows Claudia is the clumsy one with absolutely no motor skills besides the ones used for walking. But she does that rather well with the slow-motion effect and all. Ryan somehow manages to smile politely at my mother and send me a death glare at the same time.

"That is exactly how it feels like. Unfortunate."

"Thank goodness you are such a strapping young man," she says and claps him on the shoulder like he needs the encouragement. "Now take your time and walk all the way home and change, dear. Don't get all that beetroot juice in your car. It will stain." She manages to kindly manoeuvre Ryan out the kitchen entrance, far away from the rest of the party and Claudia. She even manages to close the door behind him before he has any chance of pouncing me.

She's slightly flustered and a bit out of breath, and she straightens her already straight skirt – it's an anxiety compulsion – before she turns towards me. She looks both amused and nervous, like a child who's just gotten away with doing something reckless and dangerous.

"I'm sorry about your salad, Mum," I say in order to help calm her nerves, but my mother merely shrugs.

"It's quite inedible, you know," she says casually.

"Then why did you make it?"

"Well, for Ryan, of course," she says with a delighted smile I haven't seen in years. I've missed it *so* much, and I feel a lump in my throat. Any regret I might have had towards Ryan flies out the window. My mother is happy and smiling, and I don't care about the rest. Too bad for Ryan.

CHAPTER 8

Confusion

Ryan

These first few weeks have been a bust. I've failed to win Claudia back, and until yesterday, I even failed *talking* to Claudia alone. But despite Daphne's obvious efforts, I got lucky yesterday and managed to talk to Claudia for a few minutes and persuaded her to go on a date with me in secret – only to reconnect and talk about her engagement of course. I was at the supermarket because despite living at my parents' home for the summer – meals and *company* included – I'm a grown man, and I need to make my own dinner and eat alone once in a while. Claudia was wandering the supermarket too – without a shopping basket for some reason – and it took all but three minutes to get her to agree to go out with me. That's a good sign, isn't it?

I might have managed to secure a date, but my instincts are screaming I shouldn't look forward to it because it's still more than an hour away, and that is plenty of time for Daphne to sabotage it. Desperate times and all that … so that's why Myles is with me. He doesn't know yet, and he naively believes I want to have a drink with my older brother. He should know better, really.

I need to keep track of Daphne, so I suggested to Myles we go to the pub. I'm not at all eager to get within an arm's length of her, but you know … desperate times. My face is healing nicely, and I prefer to keep it that way. Daphne is behind the bar when we enter, and I feel somewhat safer knowing there's a counter between us. Unless she's some kind of ninja she won't be able to reach me easily, but the other customers will probably get a laugh out of it if she tries. Even more, if she succeeds.

Myles glances at me and even he looks hesitant when he sits down by the bar. If we were smart, we would sit somewhere else, but I need to keep a close eye on Daphne and make certain she doesn't make a botch of my date with Claudia.

"Good evening, Daphne," Myles says politely. Apparently, he has decided to pretend he's the brave Bancroft brother today. Or maybe he just wants to be in her good graces. That ship has already sailed for me – actually, it probably went down alongside the Titanic and has found its final resting place at the bottom of the ocean.

"Myles …" She glances at me like she's considering what I'm doing here. I hardly know either because I should stay the hell away from this place when she's here.

"Daphne," I say curtly.

"Aw Ryan, you look so morose," she says with an exaggerated pout of that full lower lip I'm certain must be made for a man to suck on. She cocks her head and looks at the two of us. "Drippy and Droopy," she says and cracks up laughing at her own joke. I want to throttle her, and at least I know Myles and I are in perfect accord for once. I'm still not sure we could take her down, though. She's still giggling when she pours two glasses of local ale without us even asking for it. She's offering so I'm not paying for it, but I'm definitely drinking it.

Something's different about her, and then I realise her hair is no longer partially blue and pink. Now, all of her hair is a rich, dark brown, and it's cut in a messy asymmetrical bob with an undercut in the back. She looks like she belongs in a posh bar in London and not in a dirty pub in a primitive town with puddles and no name.

"You got a haircut," I say.

"Very observant, Ryan," she says, clearly unimpressed like she's praising a child for doing something utterly stupid. Myles glances at me.

"When did you get your nose pierced?" I ask because I suddenly see a thin silver ring in her nose.

"It came with the haircut."

"It did?" She rolls her eyes, and I cringe. I know it didn't, but I'm so surprised to see her looking like this that I can't seem to think at all.

"God, you're an idiot," she says and stalks away. Beside me, Myles groans.

"When the hell did you get so stupid around women?"

"Whenever I'm around one who's tried to end my life more than once." Myles snorts.

"Don't be ridiculous. If she'd wanted to kill you, I'm pretty sure she would've succeeded."

"You tried that for years, Drippy."

"We were children," he scoffs. "Besides, I was never quite as diabolical as she is."

"True," I acknowledge.

"So, tell me."

"Tell you what?"

"Why am I here?"

"I need a favour."

"Figured as much. You'd never invite me out for a pint otherwise." It's hard to know if he's truly disappointed or just trying to make me feel guilty. "So, what is it?"

"Keep Daphne here for a few hours."

"You must be joking," Myles exclaims, and he looks absolutely horrified. For once, I can't really blame him, and I'm not even tempted to call him a coward. Not wanting anything to do with Daphne isn't cowardness – it's common sense. "What am I supposed to do with that devilish creature for hours?"

"She likes to drink, so buy her a drink." I clap his shoulder and leave him sitting there. And ignore the curses that follow me out the door.

I'm meeting Claudia at Luciano's on the outskirts of town. It's mostly a pizza place and Halil, the Turkish owner, pretends he's a true

Italian. It's not really working out for him, but I like the man, and the food is excellent. They have linen tablecloths, and they serve the wine in high-stemmed glasses. I don't care about the rest. It's the closest thing this town has to an actual restaurant, and there's even a terrasse out back. It's rather cosy despite most of the view being blocked by Fernsby's barn. Strangely I see a large BMW in the middle of the field, and it even looks like a seven series from here. I'm just about to ask Halil about the car when Claudia comes out onto the terrasse. I asked her to meet me here because it's supposedly the most romantic place in town if you don't want to have anything to do with nature at all. Claudia definitely doesn't.

When I see her, I briefly wonder if she always looked so pale, so, so … lifeless. She air-kisses and hugs me, and I feel like I'm hugging a stranger. Maybe even a dead one. Her fingers and her body feel bony. I wonder if she's eating enough. But I suddenly remember the dress she's wearing. She had that a year ago, too, and it suited her just fine. Her movements are stiff and awkward, and she doesn't seem as graceful as she usually does. She seems almost clumsy. I wonder if she's nervous.

"Are you nervous?" I ask kindly.

"No?" She looks at me with a blank expression that would look very nice on a goldfish. Maybe she's just tired? I smile and hope it puts her at ease.

"What would you like to drink?" I ask as Halil approaches us.

"Riesling," Claudia demands and hardly looks his way. She dismisses him with a strange wave of her hand, like she's waving away a fly or trying to whip away something sticky from her fingers. It's odd and disrespectful; I even cringe, and I don't quite know what to think about it. Halil doesn't seem to care – he's probably seen worse. But still.

"Sparkling water, please," I tell him. I smile gratefully because I feel like I have to make up for Claudia's dismissal. I'm not that fond of sparkling water, but I seem to recall Claudia doesn't like the taste of beer, and there's no reason to prevent her from kissing me if that's what she wants to do. Judging by the way she looks at me I think she might.

The restaurant is busy, but Halil brings the wine and water almost immediately. Claudia quickly grabs the glass and takes a quick sip.

"That's not Riesling," she complains.

"I apologise," he says with an indulgent smile that reminds me of Mr Turner's captain. I watch Halil as he goes inside and leaves the glass on the bar. He then pours the same wine into a green, high-stemmed glass and brings it back. Claudia takes a sip, and then she nods condescendingly like she's the Queen of England.

"Much better." Confused, I look at her, and then I glance at Halil who nods seriously as he accepts the compliment. He keeps a straight face, and I almost burst out laughing because this is so bizarre.

She sloshes the wine in the glass – I thought she didn't like that – most likely in an attempt to swirl it, but her coordination seems off, and she almost spills it. I wonder if she's been drinking already, but it doesn't smell like it, and – except for a slight stiffness – she walked beautifully into the terrasse like she always does. She holds the glass on the bowl but then suddenly appears horrified, like she's appalled at the sight. She then uses both hands in order to balance the glass so she can grab the stem correctly. It looks like quite the ordeal. But the glass keeps wobbling, so she sets it down hard on the tall table. The whole exercise takes quite a while, and it looks very strange. She tries so hard to look sophisticated – at least, I think that's what she's doing – it's almost comical. The way she raises her chin, pinches her lips, almost closes her eyes, and looks over the field like she's Vivienne Leigh, and the field is Clarke Cable. She hardly seems like a real person.

I'm so confused, but nonetheless, I need to talk to her. I need to tell her why I'm back in town, and she needs to know how determined I am to get her back. But it's probably not the first thing I should tell her.

"It's good to see you, Claudia," I say with a smile.

"It's good to see you too."

"I missed you," I say.

"Well, I missed you too." It rings false to me because if she missed me, why didn't she come with me? Why didn't she call? Why didn't she do anything?

"Are you happy about your engagement?"

"Yes, very," she says. But she doesn't look happy, she looks like she doesn't care – and that's my opening.

"I'm sorry to hear that." She looks at me with a blank stare.

"Why?" she asks, but it also sounds like she's unsure if that's what she's supposed to say. It's very strange.

"Because I came back for you," I say. She brings her hands to her cheeks in an exaggerated oh-gesture I recognise from Daphne. I try not to think about it because now it makes Claudia look like a caricature. She's not supposed to look like that. Bloody Daphne!

"You did?"

"I came here to get you back." She makes another oh-gesture, and this time, I barely stop myself from laughing. Fortunately, Claudia apparently thinks I'm smiling happily.

"*Kiss* me, Ryan," she says dramatically. "Please *kiss* me." I'm momentarily stunned at the theatrics, but this is why I'm here, so I don't need to be told thrice.

I've been looking so much forward to this, but her lips are like dead pieces of meat, and when she starts moving her tongue, it's stiff and almost like a windscreen wiper. This is not how I remember kissing her feels like. Maybe it was all my imagination – and that doesn't bode well for my intentions at all.

CHAPTER 9

Misery

Daphne

Another day, another birthday. I swear people in this town only shag when the timing is right with giving birth during the summer season. Today's birthday boy is a pudgy twat. I know I shouldn't say that about a child, but he truly is. I'm absolutely certain J.K. Rowling has met this horrible child in a former life, remembered him, and created Dudley Dursley almost by copy-paste in this life. This Dudley is called Stephen, and today is his fifth birthday. Five too many if you ask me.

He has a constant pout on his face, except when he's playing with his yellow car. Then his face lights up in an evil smile I'm certain could send both Mary Poppins and Nanny McPhee running at the same time. The yellow car is apparently evil, too, because it rams hard into everything within an arm's reach. I want my own children one day, but every time I see Stephen – even from a distance – I reconsider.

To make matters worse, Claudia is delighted, and whenever Claudia is delighted, that means my life is shit. This time is no exception because while I let Myles keep me at the pub, Ryan was with Claudia at Luciano's – the most romantic place in town. Ryan was even kissing Claudia at Luciano's – the most romantic place in town, and she hasn't stopped talking about it. The next person who mentions "Luciano's – the most romantic place in town" is going to die. Violently. I happen to know where this family keeps its garden tools – shovel included.

Apparently, Ryan is the best kisser in the whole world. Looking at him, I can well believe it and I don't want to think about it. Part of me … no, that's not entirely accurate … *certain parts* of me fancies Ryan, and that's a complication I don't need. The men I'm usually interested in have left town because none of them wants their masculine ego or motorbikes involved in anybody's pink party or birthdays during the summer. In fact, they don't even want to be *seen* in town when that's taking place. So that leaves me with no sex life, and that's probably why even Ryan is starting to look good. But this is all about keeping Ryan away from Claudia and not about my neglected libido. Also, he hates me.

I give Myles the evil eye from across the room, and at least he has the decency to look slightly guilty. He knows he did wrong. Between the two brothers, Myles has the brains, while Ryan is rougher and more impulsive. I know Ryan is not stupid as such, but impulsive people often appear that way. Believe me, I know all too well, and my brother Gary often reminds me. At least Myles is hung over. He's a shitty drinker, and I sunk him easily when we started doing shots. I also held his hand and patted his forehead when he vomited in a blue bucket I snatched from the pub's storage room. Gavin is not much of a cleaner anyway, so I doubt he'll even notice it's missing. But if I'd known all Myles was doing was helping Ryan, I wouldn't have neither given him a bucket nor patted his forehead.

Stephen, the pudgy twat, is, of course, a selfish, greedy creature, so when his mother, in a far too happy voice, announces it's time for the birthday boy to have his cake, he immediately turns his attention towards her. He even drops the car because he's busy getting up so he can push his younger brother Alistair violently out of the way. Alistair lands safely on his diapered bum and immediately staggers to his feet. For a moment, I swear I see regret on Stephen's face. Probably not because he pushed Alistair, but probably because he didn't make him cry. I'm certain he's *that* kind of child and the world can't wait for this charmer to grow up and probably into something worse. For a second, Stephen looks undecided if he should give it another go to make Alistair cry, but then the cake with burning candles catches his attention. Oh great, we have a pyromaniac in the making – like his horrible personality isn't enough.

I am going to hell. I must because I don't care at all when I snatch the yellow toy car from the floor the moment he turns away. Quite the contrary, I feel a surge of satisfaction. Stephen doesn't see me doing it, but the moment he wants to invite the evil, yellow car to eat cake with him – him alone probably – he realises it's missing. He then turns into the most miserable, noisy, evil child in the world. He shrieks like a Tasmanian Devil – only louder and uglier. The horrible sound is clearly bad for Myles' headache. He winces in pain, and that makes me care about going to hell a little less. Actually, I'm starting to think I might even enjoy the ride.

Every adult gathers round the horrible child despite the volume of the twat is rising. Myles is now holding his head like he's afraid it'll burst, and just as I expected, Ryan is moving towards Claudia now that everyone – particularly his mother – is distracted. Claudia is standing at the far side of the room because she doesn't care for children or puppies or anything else that makes people turn their attention and doting to anyone but her. I get on my knees, and just as Ryan takes a step forward, I push the toy car under his foot. For a moment, I think he's actually going to succeed staying on his feet, but then, like in slow motion, he starts flapping his arms for balance. His one leg shoots out from his body like he's a cartoon character, and he lands on his ass and back with a loud thump that sounds like the air is knocked from his lungs. Nobody notices because Stephen is still screaming.

Ryan slowly gets up and I swear I see him glancing towards the thick rug only a few feet away. He probably wishes he'd landed there and not on the hard, solid wooden floor. He rubs his tailbone and delectable ass. He's limping a bit when he moves, and I *almost* feel sorry for him. Nobody saw him get hurt, and he looks rather miserable. I wonder if he hit his head, too. Also, I pity us all for having to listen not only to Stephen's screaming but also every adult in the room trying to comfort him. They sound like chickens.

Claudia is causing her own drama at the other end of the room. She has the back of her hand to her forehead and that means we're in for another dramatic performance leading up to supposedly faintness. This time is probably because of the noise and for once, I can't actually say I blame her. My father is with her and is supporting her as he leads her out of the room. Well done, Claudia! I should've come up with that – only I doubt anyone would've helped me. They'd probably just step around me and wait for me to eventually get up on my own.

The twat's cute younger brother Alistair finds the car Ryan stepped in. He looks so happy when he proudly staggers towards Stephen, offering it up. When Stephen sees the car, he stops screaming. He then uses all of his energy to punch his little brother square in the face. There's about one second where Alistair looks surprised and disappointed, and then he starts crying as blood drips from his cute little nose. And then it all starts over. Kill me now.

Stephen is making loud car noises and ramming everything, his brother is crying, and every adult in the room is cooing and trying to comfort Alistair. Claudia hasn't made it out of the room and starts whining about the noise. Outside by the garden door, an Old English Sheepdog is barking. The family's three French Bulldogs have escaped their prison in the guest room, and one is attacking the birthday cake, making adults scream and yell to make it stop. The second dog is barking at an empty armchair, and the third is shaking the TV remote to death and punching buttons while doing it. The TV turns on, the volume rises, channels shift faster and faster. Stephen's father lunges for the dog, who escapes into the garden with the remote. Myles looks like he's in pain, Ryan is hurting – too bad for him – and I'm starting to wish my family had a barn.

CHAPTER 10

Agony

Ryan

Yesterday's birthday boy was a pudgy twat. I'm probably the only person who thinks that, but he really was. That stupid yellow car was practically a tool for mutilation even before I somehow slipped in it. I didn't see her do it, but I'm certain Daphne had something to do with it. I hurt my ass and tailbone, and all in all, I haven't been bruised and in pain like this since I was in the military. Bloody Daphne.

Today is softball day, and like any man would do, I pretend I don't hurt anywhere. Men are invincible creatures, and we can definitely _not_ be brought down by a small woman.

The town can muster six softball teams, so we have a small tournament on our hands. We're divided into three pools after skills, and then we draw straws to make the teams. Luckily, I'm on the blue team, which means I'm on the same team as Claudia, while Daphne is on the red. This way, I don't have to get close to her and I'm certain I'm safer with her at a distance. Besides, she can't do anything to me today without witnesses. And I might need them when red and blue face off in the first game of the day.

Claudia insists on being right field and I wonder when she learned to throw a ball. It turns out she hasn't, but I can't bring myself to be altogether unhappy about it at first because she's standing close enough for me to see her. We're probably going to lose badly, but at least I'll have something pretty to look at.

But as the game wears on, looking at Claudia doesn't make me as happy as I thought it would. All too quickly we're down fifteen points. My competitive streak is suffering, and I'm getting slightly annoyed with Claudia. After the fiasco at Luciano's, I'm struggling with my purpose more than ever. Am I really that stupid? And even worse? I can't even blame Daphne for this.

Very fitting Daphne's is on the red team, and they're definitely out for blood. Most balls have been aimed towards the right, and every ball past first base I haven't managed to get my hands on has cost us points, because the only person behind me is Claudia. She can't run, she can't throw, she doesn't pay attention to the game – I seriously doubt she even knows it – and she spends most of the time sniffing the glove with a disgusted look on her face.

Myles steps up to the home plate, and Daphne is next in line. She looks far too comfortable with a bat in her hands. At least she's standing far away from me, and I don't think I'm in any immediate danger of being hit with the bat. Unless she decides to throw it at me.

Myles is a mediocre softball player, and I easily catch his measly attempt to target Claudia. I'm secretly far too relieved I manage to catch it before it became another hopeless task for her. When I throw the ball back to Robert Collins, who's pitching, Claudia cheers like I've just won the entire game. It's a bit misplaced simply because I threw the ball, but I still turn to her and wave. She smiles delightedly, her hair flows in the breeze, and that's when I decide she can cheer all she wants.

There's a crack of a bat hitting the ball perfectly, and then everything happens so fast. I don't even turn to look because that ball is going to be out of here by the sound of it, and not the tallest second baseman in the world could get anywhere near it. I hardly get to finish that thought when I feel it. Jesus Christ, I can't breathe! Burning pain spreads like fire from my stomach and through my body. A collective groan sounds across the softball field as I hunch over, gasping for breath. I barely manage to stay on my feet. The softball is lying on the ground in front of me, and I'm certain I see steam coming from it.

"Ouch, Ryan." Claudia and Daphne's father, John, comes rushing and lays a hand on my back. "Are you alright?" I glance up at him, but I really can't say anything yet. I feel like the ball has made a hole in my stomach, and I'm almost surprised I'm not bleeding. It feels like I've been shot with a cannonball.

"Yeah," I pant weakly through the pain.

"Daphne used to play softball in school," he says proudly.

"I think she still remembers," I moan. All of a sudden, I feel very, very, very lucky Daphne didn't throw any harder when she threw the blue ball at my groin at her aunt's birthday. I should be grateful because she could easily have unmanned me for good.

"We'd better take you to the emergency room," John concludes with a worried look on his face. I nod as I slowly and carefully stand up straight. Pain slices through my stomach and I'm still struggling to breathe properly.

"Sorry, Ryan," Daphne calls out as her father gently leads me off the field. I glance at her, and I *almost* grin at the sight of her. She's standing in her very short cut-off jeans, calm and arrogant, legs and attitude for miles. Her cap is on backwards. The bat is resting across the back of her neck, and she has one hand casually draped over the grip, the other on the barrel. If I had to be taken down by a woman, this devilish creature is the one to do it. She's definitely in a league of her own. And she's definitely out for blood.

I limp off the field. Daphne's father helps me, and he offers to take me to the hospital just in case. Maybe he's feeling guilty. *He* shouldn't, but Daphne definitely should. There's no way that hit wasn't on purpose, and even the devil, I'm certain, is a permanent fixture on Daphne's shoulder, should be feeling somewhat regretful by now.

"Good thing you're not as fragile as your brother," he says. I grimace because after coming back to town, I'm starting to feel like it. Bloody Daphne.

The drive to the emergency room takes forever because a flock of sheep has decided the main road now belongs to them, and they're not moving despite the large Range Rover. Despite the barking sheepdogs, despite the angry farmer. Daphne's father spends the time rambling off Daphne's softball statistics, and I can't help but be impressed. She didn't go to the local school, she played softball in town, so her admirable statistics isn't because she played against a goat and a duck and the retirement home. She had real competition and still did *very* well. If I'd known, I would probably not have gotten on the field with her today.

We wait for an hour and a half at the hospital, and Daphne's father is kind enough to wait with me. Hopefully he's also taking me home afterwards. When I'm finally led into an examination room, the pain has stopped burning, but it throbs about sixty-five times a minute along with my pulse. I lie down on a stretcher, and the doctor presses and tabs my stomach and abdomen.

"Do you feel faint?" I shake my head. "Any pain?"

"You're joking, right?" I ask.

"Cramps?"

"No." He brings out his stethoscope and listens to me breathe.

"Sounds normal."

"That's something," I mumble. He pulls the stethoscope out of his ears and settles it around his neck.

"Nothing wrong as far as I can tell. You can go home, but keep an eye out for blood in your urine. Come back if you vomit and there's blood. Keep an eye on your stool. If anything looks out of the ordinary, come back." I feel speechless, but I still manage to ask:

"You're joking?"

"Not at all."

So, now I need to stare at my own shit. Bloody Daphne.

CHAPTER 11

Broken

Ryan

It's been a few days since the softball game, and I have a bruise bigger than my palm on my stomach. It's tender and a marvellous palette of the darkest colours of hell courtesy of Daphne the Devil. My shit is looking fine, by the way.

Most of all, I want to lie down in a foetal position, but I'm not giving up on Claudia, and I'm not accepting defeat to a five-foot woman. So, when I arrive at the function room for Christina and Leslie's engagement party, I straighten my back and pretend I'm bloody James Bond on a mission in enemy territory. If Daniel Craig could pull it off in Macau, then so can I in Puddle-whatever-town!

Leslie's parents own the function rooms, and it's clear Christina and Leslie still know how to party. The music is blaring out from small basement windows, and I see blue and green lights flickering, too. A pony and a goat are tied to the flagpole. Leslie used to host the best and wildest parties, and her parents didn't care – as long as we stayed in the basement and as long as nobody brought any animals inside. By the looks of it, nothing has changed.

Christina is a beautiful blonde who could easily conquer the runway, but she loves the country and this town in particular for some unknown reason. She lived in London for a while but decided to come back here. I know her from school, and I was somewhat heartbroken when I found out she didn't like boys *at all*. Most of us boys were. I think that's got to be the only time Myles and I agreed on anything in our teenage years. We spent an entire night talking about how amazing boys – particularly the two of us – were and what she was missing out on. Us, of course. When she started dating Leslie, we had the same conversation all over again because Leslie was missing out on us, too. Both of them were party girls and both of them were the ones every boy in school had a crush on. As far as I know, they're still party girls, so at least tonight should be fun.

When I enter the basement, ABBA is playing, and it's impossible for me not to smile at the sound of it. Their music is truly amazing, and I enjoy every tune, at least until the beautiful build-up of "Don't Shut Me Down" is ruined by Daphne, who comes out of nowhere and grabs my hand.

"Dance with me, Ryan," she demands, and I follow her to the dancefloor. Daphne is dangerous, so I feel compelled to do as she asks. Her hand feels soft and warm, and it's hard to believe those delicate fingers can break bones and wield a bat – and God knows what else – like a murder weapon.

I don't see Claudia, and I don't even know if she's going to be here, so why not waste some time dancing with Daphne? It seems highly unlikely I'm going to make peace with her, but maybe if I entertain her and talk to her for a while, she might run screaming?

Maybe I can annoy her so much she doesn't want to be close to me ever again, not even close enough to hurt me. She can still hurt me from a distance, though, she's proven that already. But she wouldn't do anything at a dancefloor, would she? Still, I hesitate because, knowing Daphne, she might just create an opportunity for her to headbutt me – I'm not sure my nose can take anymore at this point. It's already broken but I'm certain Daphne easily can demolish any healing process going on in my face.

She's dressed in a sixties-style cherry red dress and looks like she could be in "Dirty Dancing". She moves like it, too, rhythmically and sensuously. Her body promises a man endless pleasure – too bad she's also almost lethal. At the moment, she's fortunately having fun with something else than mutilation, and I truly appreciate that. I've never danced with a woman like this, and it's never been this fun, either. I forget all about my initial plan to annoy her because it's fascinating seeing her like this. She's smiling and having fun and there's no doubt in my mind she loves to dance. When "Does Your Mother Know" comes on, I'm having one hell of a good time, and I don't even pretend I'm going to let her go.

"You like to dance?" I ask loudly to be heard over the music.

"Yes!" she says with a contagious smile I can't help returning. "If the DJ plays 'You Never Can Tell', you'd better know your 'Pulp Fiction' and your twist," she says like she's certain I will actually go along with it. I probably will because apparently, dancing with a creature from hell can be fun. Maybe it's adrenalin because of the dash of fear I feel?

Some idiot, I think is Myles' childhood friend, claims Daphne's attention for "Waterloo". I shouldn't be annoyed about it; I really shouldn't – I should be relieved – but nonetheless, I am. I escape the dancefloor – only it doesn't feel like an escape, but a dismissal. I'm going to get Daphne back – I flinch at the phrase – and I know exactly how. Determined, I make my way to the DJ booth through the crowd. It's not as easy as it sounds because I grew up in this useless town, and I still know a lot of people here. I like most of them, too, but right now, I am on a mission. Daniel Craig definitely did better than me.

Leslie's older sister Brittany abruptly pulls me to the dancefloor to "Runaround Sue". She's a great dancer, but all I can think about is how I'd rather have danced with Daphne. I see her across the dancefloor with her father, and they look like they're having the time of their lives. It looks like a swing but without the lifts and flips.

Daphne's father is a large man. He usually wears pastels, striped shirts, and braces, and it makes him look slightly silly. His movements are usually slobby and almost like he doesn't know how to properly control his own body. But tonight, on the dance floor, wearing a suit, he looks like a different man. He's confident and charismatic and has an energy I've never seen with him before. He looks younger somehow, too. It doesn't escape my notice that Claudia isn't there

clinging to either him or Gemma, who's clearly tipsy and happily
sipping a very large and colourful cocktail at the bar.

I haven't paid much attention to Brittany during our dance – I've
been looking at Daphne – but she seems happy enough and hugs me
afterwards. She's also slightly drunk and giggly, so I have no illusion
I've given her the attention I ought to. I just couldn't keep my eyes
away from Daphne for some reason.

Determined yet again, I move towards the DJ booth. "Waterloo"
turns out to have been the last of ABBA and "Runaround Sue" was
only the first song in what turns out to be an absurd mix of music
genres. When I finally get to the booth, I see a miserable-looking DJ,
who's covering his ears and clearly suffering under the strange mix
of music as well.

"Hey Mark," I shout at the DJ.

"Hey, Ryan." He holds out his hand with a big smile, and I must
admit it's not so bad being back in town when I meet some of my old
friends. "Welcome back. What do you need?"

"Do you take requests?"

"Only for another twenty-three and a half minutes. Then I get to
go back to doing my job properly." I laugh at this because Mark
detests it when he can't decide absolutely *every* single piece of music
being played – he always has. I don't blame him, though, because it
can be rather difficult blending a Dolly Parton ballad seamlessly with

2 Unlimited. The ABBA extravaganza that was no doubt Mark's doing was so much better. "So, what do you want?" he asks.

"Never Can Tell."

"I hope you mean the song," he says warningly. He doesn't look like he's in the mood for *any* jokes at the moment.

"I do."

"I got a few requests before yours."

"Fair enough. I can wait."

"After 'How Am I Supposed to Live Without You'."

"Michael Bolton? That's horrible," I exclaim.

"True. And very noisy. I suggest you go outside to take a piss for a very long time."

"Don't tell me … Mrs Kensington?"

"Yeah, says it's 'their song'."

"No wonder their marriage is shit." Mark grins and gives me the thumbs up. "Any chance you can get me an intro?"

"To your song?" I nod. "Yeah, okay, I'll figure something out," he says and he's already tapping away on his laptop when I walk away.

Contrary to what a smart man would do, I don't go outside while Michael Bolton – painfully in more ways than one – cries his heart out, I stay inside. There's an odd feeling of anticipation thrumming in me that I'm not ready to consider too much. I casually make my way towards Daphne, and I feel an odd rush of excitement when the intro from the movie's twist contest rings out.

"Ladies and gentlemen, now's the moment you've all been waiting for. The world-famous Jack Rabbit Slim's Twist Contest. Now this is where one lucky couple will win this handsome trophy that Marilyn here is holding. Now, who will be our first contestants?" Most people here look confused, but Daphne squeals delightedly. She glances around and when she sees me, her face lights up in a heart-stopping smile. The cherry red lipstick emphasises her plump lips, and I've given up counting how many times I've thought about sucking on them. It would probably get me killed somehow. She quickly bends to unstrap her shoes. I don't think, I don't hesitate, I just kick off my shoes as well and drag her to the dancefloor as quickly as possible.

Impressively, Daphne has more attitude than Uma Thurman, but if anyone could pull that off, it would certainly be her. It's very fitting, considering Daphne probably has a "death list five", too. *At least* five. Knowing Daphne, I'll be "Bill" on that list, but I have no illusions that she'll save me for last. In fact, she has already started killing me slowly.

People join us, and there's cheering and whistling. One even shouts, "Go Uma," and I'm certain we'd win if we actually were at Jack Rabbit Slim's. Despite we do our best to mimic the push and pull in the movie choreography there is no push. Only pull. Whatever is happening, Daphne is pulling me in – how is that even possible? Maybe because her movements are not stiff and clumsy but casual and natural. And so bloody sexy. She seems so … so real. I am *not* comparing her and Claudia!

I almost want to hug her when the dance ends because I feel like we're partners who put on some kind of show that went well, and we should celebrate – and besides, it was fun. I want to hold her hand to help her keep her balance when she straps on her high heels again because I feel like that's the gentlemanly thing to do. And I want her on my arm when we get something to drink because I don't want to let go of her. I don't quite know how to deal with that, so I do none of those things.

Apparently, Claudia has finally decided to show up, and when I catch a glimpse of her in the wardrobe, I have a strange feeling of guilt and maybe even a little bit of regret. Daphne is the one who's supposed to feel guilty after all she's done to me. Only, and this is strange, I feel guilty towards *Daphne*. I have absolutely no idea why, and it doesn't make any sense at all.

Claudia barely manages to greet Christina and Leslie politely and I inwardly cringe. Christina is considered the most beautiful woman not only in town, but also in a hundred miles radius. Claudia hates it and says she only "tolerates" Christina's presence because she's a lesbian. I've never understood jealousy and the bitching that comes with it. Rumour has it that Christina has kissed Daphne – thoroughly

– because she had a crush on her. Claudia found it disgusting for some reason. Rumour has it Daphne had laughed about it and admitted it was a pretty good kiss, but she still liked boys. I am *not* comparing Daphne and Claudia!

Just as Claudia steps into the room, Daphne takes a step back, and in an instant, the hellhound sheds its woman costume, and everything is back to normal as she steps on my toes. I clench my teeth, but the excruciating pain of Daphne's pointed heel makes me groan anyway. I've never broken any toes before, but somehow, I have no doubt that's what just happened. A strange sound, a pinch, and then a throbbing pain. I force myself to keep standing, but most of all, I want to sink to my knees and cry out. Viggo Mortensen, I feel you.

Daphne doesn't seem to notice, and she eagerly grabs my father's hand when he offers it. They disappear to the dancefloor while I'm still clenching my teeth in pain. I don't make it to Claudia. In fact, I don't even try. I retrieve to one of the tables near the stairs instead. I sit down, and I'm tempted to take off my shoe because I can't feel my toes, but I doubt any kind of inspection will make me feel any better. Besides, I'm not certain I can even bring myself to put the shoe back on. And the last thing I need is to be limping about wearing only one shoe when Daphne is around. It'd be like cutting yourself with a knife in shark-infested waters.

At least Daphne is not circling me for an imminent attack. She's on the dancefloor with my father, who spins her to "She Works Hard for the Money". She looks like she's having a hard time not no laugh. My father acts like he thinks he was Fred Astaire in his former life – he definitely wasn't – and my mother refuses to do anything but slow dance with him, so Daphne probably just made his night. Somehow, she even makes him look better than he usually does. Not that it takes that much.

The print on that blasted sexy cherry red dress she's wearing almost makes it look like lace, and that's another image I don't want in my head: Daphne wearing cherry red lacy lingerie that matches the lipstick I want to lick of her lips. I must be a masochist because I have no doubt it would be painful somehow. But for some reason, everything inside me is completely on board with this idea as I watch her. God, I'm stupid! I have absolutely no idea where Claudia is.

I get up – reluctantly – because I need to clear my head. I need air! And maybe I can even yell out some of the confusion, pain, and frustration in the nearest bush. Absentminded, I don't place my foot properly on the concrete step. At the pain pounding through my broken toes, I lose my balance. I stumble forward, and before I know it, I bang my head hard against the stainless-steel railing. I land on my arm a few steps further up the stairs, and I immediately know something is wrong. Again. The sound of a snap gives it away – and then the pain. I groan and curse myself for not staying quiet when I see Myles, who's standing nearby, turn towards me.

"Jesus, Ryan, are you that drunk already?" I send him a glare that's probably not as evil as I intended because he comes rushing to me instead of running away. "What happened?" he asks and manages to sound adequately concerned.

"I think I probably just broke my arm," I say through clenched teeth.

"What?" He glances nervously at the arm I'm now cradling to my chest.

Myles is a wimp, no doubt about it. Blood, bruises, pain, anything worse than a cuticle, really, and he starts to look green. None the less, he takes me to the emergency room. He hates any party that involves dancing because, most of all, he just looks hilarious. He's like Hugh Grant in "Love Actually", but without the charm, enjoyment, and confidence that kind of ridiculous dance act requires. That's probably another reason he was quite happy I got hurt. At least, as long as he doesn't have to look at the damage.

The nurse is a young man called Thomas. He takes one look at the strange bump on my arm and then schedules an X-ray immediately.

"Could you please X-ray my foot as well?" I ask.

"What happened to your foot?"

"Think I might have broken a few toes." He glances at my face, which – apart from tonight's damage – is healing nicely but still looks slightly bruised.

"What on Earth did you get into?"

"It's a long story," I say and Myles snickers. I knew I should have left him at the party. Too bad he has proven himself useful driving the car here.

"Do you know Daphne Fletcher?" Myles asks and the bloody idiot is struggling not to burst out laughing. The nurse looks at me in wonder.

"I thought *you* were the tough one," Thomas says as he turns towards me. "Weren't you in the military?" Yes, but the military doesn't make Jason Bournes – that happens in the SAS. People should really know this. Myles hates it whenever he's described as the wimpy brother one way or another. I, on the other hand, relish it. And it's not like Thomas is wrong. I shoot Myles a triumphant smile before I answer Thomas.

"That was years ago," I tell him. "And do you honestly think the armed forces can compete with an emissary from the deepest pits of hell?" He chuckles and shakes his head.

"True. Nothing compares to Daphne." He's right – nothing compares to her. And it's starting to drive me just a little bit insane.

Thomas has just finished dabbing the scratch above my eyebrow – courtesy of the steel railing – with some kind of antiseptic that feels like it's based on acid. Maybe I *am* wimpy – but I keep that thought to myself. The doctor who comes in to look at my X-rays is the same one who inspected my stomach after Daphne hit me with the softball.

"Ryan Bancroft. Again."

"Again," I confirm.

"Are you in trouble with someone?" he asks seriously. In trouble? You can say that again. But I don't think a tiny woman is what he means. He's probably wondering if we have any local bikers or gangs of criminals he hasn't heard of.

"Daphne Fletcher."

"Ah," he says and nods. I suppose this makes sense to him because Daphne must have been responsible for several patients during the years. Knowing Daphne, she's probably the reason the doctor keeps busy and still has a job.

"Is it very bad?" Myles asks as the doctor looks at the X-rays.

"We have to realign the bone," the doctor answers casually. Realigning a bone is not as bad and particularly not as gory as it sounds, but it's enough to make Myles queasy, which pleases me immensely. He *is* the wimpy brother, no matter how hard he tries not to be. That makes me very happy at the moment.

"I'll wait outside," he says and rushes out the room. He'll probably be looking for the nearest bin where he can throw up.

So, thanks to Daphne, I now have a broken arm, and judging by the throbbing in my face, I'll have another black eye in the morning. Bloody Daphne.

CHAPTER 12

Guilt

Daphne

Regrets. I'm starting to have them – I'm feeling slightly guilty, too – and that's *not* something that happens often. For some reason, Ryan must really want my sister since he's not discouraged by either her personality or anything that has happened to him. I think even his wellies need bandages by now. The only thing I absolutely don't regret is pushing him into the water because when he finally got out, all his clothes were sticking to him like glue … hello, hot stuff. From this day on, simply for my own viewing pleasure, I'll push him into any kind of water any day, anywhere I get the chance, whether he ends up with Claudia or not.

Claudia will be back in town tomorrow. She has been away for a week, and that has given Ryan time to heal – particularly since he's stayed far away from me. I didn't imagine stepping on his toes would break two of them and be the catalyst for a broken arm and another black eye. I haven't seen it, but of course, it's all over town like actual breaking news. I keep telling myself that, technically, it's not my fault he broke his arm. It's not really working, though. I still feel guilty.

The Met Office has issued a storm warning. They predict major risk of structural damages, floods, and power cuts. Flights will probably be cancelled, and schools and bridges will be closed as a precaution. Gavin has decided to close the pub, too, and he has also decided now would be an excellent time for me to clean the place properly for once. He usually only finds that important when he's been tipped off an inspection is coming. Besides, Gavin dares not risk any of the heavy drinkers with no money getting stranded in the pub. I get paid, so I don't mind cleaning. And being here alone lets *me* be in total control of the sound system and not the regulars who refuse to recognise there's any music besides The Beatles.

To me, it's completely impossible to clean without singing – or dancing when I'm not carrying water or standing on a ladder with a duster. I can still shake my ass on the ladder, though. So, when I wash the floor, I dance and probably do things with the mop it had never imagined. I don't need to be Snow White to have my own Prince Buckethead, and I pretend I'm not imagining anyone in particular. *He* probably thinks I'm Cinderella's ugly sister. I ignore that thought as I dance and sway my hips. I love to feel the skirt whirling around my knees, but I'm going to hate that when I eventually go outside – I'm going to look like Marylin Monroe on that subway grate. Only Mud-fucking-Puddletown is nowhere near New York and I'm no Marilyn. I'm going to look like shit even without wellies. My flat is not far, but if the storm picks up, as they've said, I may have to spend the night on the couch in the backroom. It's disgusting and I really don't want to think about what it's been used for – neither before nor after Gavin found it in the street.

For my own amusement, I've made a storm playlist. Earth *Wind & Fire* is there with "September", "Let's Groove", and "Boogie Wonderland". Of course, "It's Raining Men" and "Thunderstruck". "Like a Hurricane", "Crying Lightning", and "Have You Seen the Rain". Billy Joel's "Storm Front" would've been the obvious choice, only it's not that fun to dance to. I went with "We Didn't Start the Fire" from the Storm Front album and hope it's not an omen that lightning will strike a fire will start, and the pub will burn down. Lyrics in the first verse contain Marilyn Monroe – it's definitely going to be the song I'm singing if I go home. Outside, thunder is *rolling* … hmm … I should've snuck "Proud Mary" on the playlist too.

I can't help pressing repeat when "Heat Wave" comes on. It's not really storm-appropriate, but I really love it, and it almost distracts me from the howling of the wind and the creaking of the building. It's a clear sign the storm is definitely coming – and I'm not only talking about the one who's knocking on the door to the pub just now. The place is closed and empty because everyone is at home securing trampolines and plastic garden furniture. But for some reason, Ryan Bancroft, of all people, is standing outside the pub.

"Are you here to kill me?" I ask as I open the door. Ryan glares at me and pushes past me into the pub. The storm is already raging, and I struggle to close the door. Ryan's hair is damp, a complete mess and he looks like he just rolled out of bed. No reason to think about that, really.

"Tempting, but no. Why?"

"Those wellies look like you're a murderer in a horror movie," I say and point towards his wellies. They're big and black and look like the perfect footwear if you're getting knee-deep in blood. All he needs is a fisherman's ice hook to complete the picture.

"Not yet," he says and glares at me.

"You know there's a storm coming, right?"

"Of course, I know. I'm not an idiot," he snaps.

"Then what are you doing here? Going out seems rather *idiotic*."

"My mother sent me to make sure *poor Daphne* has managed to close down the pub and is not caught in the storm," he sneers. "Because with a bloody broken arm and two broken toes, I'm the best person in the world to help you with anything that requires physical labour. Considering I preferably shouldn't be walking about at all!"

"Then limp back home, Gimpy."

"It's your fault, I'm limping."

"You are the worst chinless wonder this town has ever seen," I yell.

"I bloody hate you," he roars. "How can something so simple as walking into a pub in this ridiculously primitive town with no name become the biggest regret of my whole sodding life?" He holds on to his head like it's about to explode, and he's trying to keep it together. I'm actually quite impressed he hasn't thrashed me yet. Woman or not.

"The feeling is mutual," I shout. "Why the hell do you think I hit you?!"

"I want to punch you so bloody much."

"Then why don't you?"

"I don't hit women. I told you that already."

"Poor you," I mock. I have absolutely no idea why I keep provoking him except my feelings are getting away from me again because I feel frustrated for some reason. Ryan ignores me.

"My physical health is failing faster than good intentions around you. By the end of the season, I'll be in a wheelchair with PTSD."

"Don't be a cream puff," I snort.

"You're turning me into Myles," he roars. I almost laugh. Almost. But I can't. Ryan looks furious and very *un*-cream puff-like. He looks dangerous. He looks gorgeous and wild. My heart is pounding, the pulse is thundering in my ears, and my breathing is fast. There's something crackling in the air, and it's not the lightning outside. It feels like Martha & The Vandellas' heat wave has made it inside the pub because I suddenly feel warm all over.

I recognise my frustration for what it is: I want Ryan. Shocked by that realisation I don't answer him, but just stand there gawking at him. Surprised at my silence, he looks at me, and that's when things turn really strange. I meet him halfway as he grabs me, and his lips slam onto mine. I almost expect him to push me away, but he doesn't. I suppose I should feel guilt towards Claudia, but as it is, she's engaged to another man and nothing I do with Ryan should concern her. This *is* happening. Too bad for Claudia.

CHAPTER 13

Passion

Ryan

I vaguely notice how small Daphne feels in my arms. Small but strong. Curvy and far softer than I've imagined. And yes, I have certainly imagined it. More and more often. Dancing with her only left me dissatisfied that I couldn't feel her up like I wanted to. Couldn't touch her like I yearned to do – like I was *supposed* to do. Daphne is meant for me to touch like I'm doing now.

During the past year, whenever I was thinking about kissing Claudia again, I always imagined soft lips and tongue, scalding passion, but the reality wasn't like that at all. When I've considered kissing Daphne – honestly, I have – I've imagined kissing a razor-covered boulder, but this isn't like that at all, either. I suck on that full lower lip, and I was right – it *is* made for a man to suck on. I bite it gently, and she moans into my mouth, making my cock harden even further. This devilish creature turns me so much on I can't believe it. Flashes of her smile, of her dancing, and her running around on senior's market day run through my mind and I feel a strange surge of happiness that only fuels my lust.

I grab her ass, and her legs wrap around me like just they're supposed to. Our kissing is deep and hungry and rough, and still, it's not enough. The craving inside me feels like an animal struggling to get out – and I let it. Daphne rubs her tits against my chest and pulls my hair. I don't feel the pain from the hair pulling, and I don't feel my broken toes or my bruised body either. God, I want her. And I'm going to get her.

She gasps when I slam her back against the wall, but it doesn't slow either of us down. She grinds against me, and it feels like I black out for a second or two before my mind finally surfaces again. I tear my jeans open to release my cock, that's hard and eager for a trip into the deepest pit of hell. I pull her tiny knickers to one side, and then I plunge. In more ways than one.

Jesus Christ, she feels good. Tight, soft, wet, amazing. There's a faint hint of arousal in the air, and I almost feel like I've been drugged by the most powerful aphrodisiac. I'm probably going to come within seconds, and that'll be yet another thing for Daphne to throw at me later. At least it won't hurt me physically. Shivers run up my spine and my entire body is tingling. I'm dangerously close to losing my mind, and only a tiny part of my brain points out I shouldn't be doing this. Fortunately, there's no room for thoughts because my cock has just auctioned off my sanity and my common sense, and it appears Daphne made a bargain because they sure went quick and cheap.

Daphne has absolutely no hesitation and no doubt. It's just pure lust, and suddenly, I love she's impulsive and doesn't seem to think at all. And it doesn't feel stupid. It feels right. Every hard thrust into her, every slow pull out. The wooden wall creaks when I push her against it harder and faster when my fucking turns hectic. I'm buried to the hilt inside her, but I still want more. I want everything. Even the rumoured bitemarks.

Her T-shirt is slightly damp, and I know she was working hard on cleaning the place when I got here, but that only increases my desperation. This is sweaty and dirty and rough fucking, and it's so bloody perfect. With her, anything less would have been a disappointment. Thankfully, she's got her legs wrapped around my hips since I can only hold her up using one hand. I support the cast on the wall over her head, and it works out perfectly to get even closer to her.

"Ryan …" She moans my name, and a shiver runs up my spine despite my sweating and panting.

"Shut up, Daphne," I groan. And what do you know … for once, she does. At least for a second until she comes around my cock. It rings out like a shiver in my soul.

"Oh-oh-oh-oh-oh."

"Fuuuuck." I roar. I pant, and I keep thrusting as I come.

The cast on the wall is the only thing that keeps me upright as I slowly open my eyes. Daphne is in my arms, and her legs are wrapped around my hips. We're both breathing hard; the air is filled with our mixed scent of perfume, sweat, and come. I pull out of her, and she slowly puts her feet on the floor.

This was not supposed to happen, and we both know it. But when I finally meet Daphne's eyes nothing has changed with her. There's no doubt, no hesitation. And I'll probably get hurt at some point.

"You'd better not be finished for the night," she says threateningly as she grabs my sweater and pulls me toward the room in the back. I stumble after her with my jeans around my knees. She doesn't need to worry; I'm nowhere near finished with her.

"You wish," I growl and pull her to me to kiss her roughly. I'm going to fuck the living hell out of her even if it kills me. Even if I have to ask Myles to drive me to the emergency room again afterwards. He should get a laugh out of that, and it'll be all worth it.

The backroom has a disgusting-looking couch; it's slightly damp, and there's a draught too. I don't give a shit because something is far more important right now. More kissing. More touching. More skin. More everything. Frantic hands tear clothes and rip it off. I hardly notice. But I notice how Peter Driben lacked the perfect model – Christ, she's gorgeous.

I don't want to think about how much alcohol has been spilt on the couch, how many drugs have been taken, or how many people have had sex here before us. I don't care either because I want to let out all my pent-up aggression. I want to punish her for all the pain she's inflicted on me. Most of all, I want to punish her for making me doubt everything. To long for something I shouldn't want. Something I'm not *supposed* to want.

"Get on your knees," I demand. She's hardly made it to her knees and spread her legs before I line up my cock and hammer into her. I'm not worried because she can take it – I know she can. She hits like a pro boxer, and she carries cases of ale up from the basement. There's nothing frail about Daphne, not the way she talks, hits, and apparently fucks. *This* is how she's supposed to look like: on her knees, me fucking her, her moaning my name, surrendering to me. I smack her ass, the sound sends shivers up my spine, and I wish to God I had the use of both my hands.

As it turns out, I don't need both my hands to hold her close. Daphne takes and demands everything I've got, and she doesn't surrender anything to me, only to pleasure. At least I'm the one giving it to her. That's got to count for something.

*

By early morning the storm outside has abated. But there's definitely a new one building momentum inside my head despite it feels like my mind has been blown, struck by lightning, and the remains scattered by the storm. I've only just pulled out of her – for the third time since I got here last night – when she kicks my shin.

"Get the fuck out, Ryan," she says with a content sigh that's almost a moan.

"Yeah, yeah, I'm going." I smack her ass hard as I get up and look for my clothes. She lazily covers herself with a plaid and curls up on the couch and closes her eyes. She looks like she'll be asleep within minutes. Lucky her.

In the pub's main room "Heat Wave" is still playing, like it's been doing all night. There's no doubt the song is going to remind me of Daphne and the night we've just spent together for the rest of my life.

I'm exhausted when I leave the pub. I can't remember when's the last time I felt like this. When was the last time I spent hours with a woman like this? Felt like this? Have I ever? My clothes were scattered all over the place, my shirt was torn, and, of course, I'm now sporting bite marks. Despite her short nails, I know I have marks from them on my ass too. This was definitely a mistake. Unfortunately, she's also the best shag I've ever had. I didn't even consider a condom, and with my luck, she'll give birth to a litter of hellhounds in a couple of months. Bloody Daphne.

CHAPTER 14

Surprise

Ryan

Claudia is back in town from a, according to my mother – who's probably the *least* reliable source in this case – romantic getaway in Birmingham with Arthur, and I'm not quite certain how I feel about that. She has only just arrived home a few hours ago, and now she's invited me to her parent's house. I have absolutely no idea why, and I'm not as eager to go as I thought I'd be. And as predicted a storm is raging in my head.

I couldn't tell if Claudia was happy or sad when she called, mostly, she was just indifferent. Isn't she always? She definitely lacks Daphne's temper and dedication. I don't know what I hope for, either. Do I want to hear she had an awful time on her getaway and regrets she's not with me? Or do I want to hear how happy she is with Arthur, and I have no chance of winning her back? I honestly don't know. I don't know anything anymore.

Claudia asked me to let myself in when I got to her parents' house, and I do. Only I don't know what to expect. She's not exactly the type to invite a man over and await him in the bedroom wearing only lingerie, so what is it? But what I was *not* expecting was to see a group of people when I enter the living room. Myles, my parents, Claudia's parents, and her brother. My parents are sitting on the couch; they look slightly confused and very uncomfortable. My mother, in particular, of course. Nothing throws my mother off-kilter as being near Claudia.

When she sees me, Claudia moves towards me. Her hair flows behind her, but for the first time, I notice how she moves her head awkwardly from side to side to give it an extra swing. I've never noticed that before and it looks sort of ridiculous. She grabs my arm. It feels awkward somehow, and she feels wrong too. She's too skinny, and her fingers feel like claws. She smells wrong. She looks wrong. Everything feels wrong – and not only this strange situation where everyone is staring at her and me like we've just performed an awful circus act, and they can't bring themselves to clap. Not even to be polite.

"We're getting married this Saturday," Claudia says delightedly.

"Yes, we know, dear," her father says patiently. Until recently, I hadn't noticed how much people around Claudia always seem to strive for patience. And even worse? I understand them completely.

"How do you know?" she pouts. "You ruined the surprise."

"Honey, we were there when Arthur proposed," her mother says soothingly. "We all were."

"Oh," she says happily. "Well, I'm not marrying Arthur. I'm marrying Ryan," she declares. My father starts coughing, and my mother stares at us with wild eyes. Her hand is trembling and she's clenching her sherry glass so hard I think it might shatter. Myles rolls his eyes so violently that I think they might actually get stuck. If they do, I still have a chance of locking him up at the ripe age of thirty-two. And me? My insides turn cold, and I suddenly feel slightly nauseous.

"That's not possible, dear," her mother says politely.

"Why not? We've already booked the church for my wedding with Arthur. I'll just have another groom."

"Sweetheart, you can't do that," her father says patiently, like a man who has years of experience dealing with preposterous episodes and stupid comments. He probably has. Driving me to the emergency room during the softball game was probably the least of it.

"This isn't Las Vegas, dear. You have to give notice to the register office," her mother says, and she sounds almost regretful.

"So, give it."

"Twenty-eight days." Yeah, that's definitely regret in her mother's voice.

"I won't wait that long."

"You have to."

"No, I don't. We *are* getting married this Saturday," she insists and furiously stomps her foot like a five-year-old.

"We are?" I ask when I force myself to speak. She looks at me like I've missed the point of the entire conversation. Maybe I have.

"Well, yes. You said you came back for me."

"What about Arthur?" her mother asks.

"What about him?" Claudia asks and looks genuinely confused. How can she discard him so easily? Probably the same way she discarded me. "Well, he can come to the wedding if you insist. If he wants to," she says with a shrug when she notices everyone keeps looking at her. Her parents glance at each other, Gary is trying to look like the superior adult in the room, and my parents sit on the couch looking shell-shocked. Myles is struggling to contain his smirk, but he's doing a piss poor job of it. I have absolutely no idea which part of this travesty that makes him so happy. From his point of view there must be several reasons to choose from.

"I think we should just forget about this whole thing," Claudia's mother says and claps her hands enthusiastically. She looks frantically around the living room like she's missing something important. "Where's Daphne?"

"Why do you care?" Gary asks.

"I need Daphne."

"No, you don't. She's too impulsive for any adult and rational discussion."

"No, she isn't," their mother insists.

"Well, then it's her actions that are just plain stupid," Gary scoffs like it's the only other possibility. I glance at him, and I might not want to hit Daphne, but I definitely want to hit him.

"Don't say that," their father grumbles.

"She is stupid," Gary insists. "She's barely an adult."

"I want Daphne here," his mother insists, sounding more and more nervous and uncomfortable.

"This has nothing to do with Daphne," Gary snaps.

"Yes, it has. I made her promise to keep Ryan away from Claudia."

"You what?" I ask disbelievingly, just as Claudia whines:

"Why would you do that?"

"To make sure you got married to Arthur, of course," her mother says vaguely. Something's amiss here. There's definitely something Claudia's mother isn't telling. "I didn't want Ryan to ruin it," she admits quietly.

"Now wait a minute …" my father roars. "Are you saying Ryan's not good enough for your daughter?"

"*Sit down*, Anthony," my mother hisses through clenched teeth. If anything, she doesn't want me and Claudia together in any way, and my father's battered family pride is certainly not allowed to interfere with that. As expected, her glass of sherry is drained. It's probably licked clean, too. At least it isn't shattered.

"But I want to marry Ryan this Saturday," Claudia whines.

"You can't."

"I want to." She stomps her foot and that's all it takes for Claudia's mother to finally lose her patience.

"Claudia, just get married and move out already!" she snaps. "At this point, I don't even care *who* you marry. As long as it's soon."

"What?" Claudia asks, baffled.

"I can't take it anymore," her mother says. She gets up and starts pacing back and forth in the living room. We all look at her like we're at Wimbledon, watching the ball go back and forth over the net. She rubs her temples, and she looks so exhausted I'm starting to feel sorry for her. Somebody should comfort her, calm her down, get her a glass of wine, a cup of tea, or something to make her feel better. I can't help wondering if that's what Daphne would've done if she'd been here.

"What do you mean?" Claudia asks. She sounds like a child, and she's completely oblivious to her mother's obvious distress. I'm certain Daphne wouldn't have been.

"The drama," Claudia's mother says tiredly and finally, she stops wringing her hands. "The endless, endless drama. Faking happiness each and every time you have a new fiancée. Faking sadness each and every time you break it off. Comforting you when you're hysterical. Planning another wedding, cancelling another wedding. Calling the vicar, calling off the caterers, spending all our money on food we'll never eat. Paying for function rooms, we'll never use."

"Well, this time, it's in a garden too," Claudia says delightedly. Her mother sighs deeply.

"If you want Ryan, then have him. I don't care anymore. I just want it to stop!" Gemma's voice cracks at the end, and I truly feel sorry for her. My mother lets out a strangled whimper, and my father grabs her hand like he, too, fears the outcome of this conversation.

Claudia's father looks down and starts rubbing his forehead like he is completely worn out and has a headache. I think he has, and I think it has a name. Claudia looks stunned, and then she turns to me expectantly, and I know what she is going to say even before she utters:

"Las Vegas?"

I now have what I came back for. I only have to buy the plane tickets.

CHAPTER 15

Disappointment

Daphne

As soon as I enter my parent's house that afternoon my father comes running into the hallway.

"Quick, Daphne, get out," he whispers with some kind of urgency. I'm too stunned to do anything but follow him as he grabs my hand, yanks open the front door and ushers me outside. He's breathing hard and almost looks like he has just escaped the Armageddon.

"Dad, what's going on?"

"Drama. You just missed it." I sigh in relief because, for a moment, I almost thought we were escaping a hostage situation or a home robbery. This is equally bad but not potentially deadly. Probably not – except I might've ended up killing someone if I'd been involved in any more drama.

"Claudia wants to elope to Las Vegas and get married." He snickers, and that is so unlike my father I immediately start worrying about his mental health. Maybe Claudia has finally pushed both our parents over the edge?

"What? Elope? Why? She's marrying him this weekend."

"No, not Artur. Ryan ..." He says something else, but I hardly hear it. My stomach twists, and my entire body feels burning hot and then ice cold. I can't catch my breath, and I'm feeling dizzy. Looking at my father I know he's giving an animated narrative about everything that just happened, but I can't hear anything. I don't want to.

I panic, and then I flee.

I run through town, and I vaguely hear people calling my name, but I don't stop. I don't care for small talk or cheeky remarks. All I care about is the pain I feel. I've seen the tattoo on Ryan's arm – it's an amazing griffin – I've licked it too. Also, I might have bitten it. I've run my fingers through the hairs on his chest and stomach when he dozed off for a few minutes. I lay there, and for a moment, that disgusting couch was the best place in the world. And for a moment, I pretended he was mine. I pretended I wasn't the ugly sister but someone a man like him wanted to be with – and not only shag for a night. Someone he'd even want to keep.

I know the sex in the pub didn't really mean anything, but somehow it did anyway. To me, at least. Stupid, impulsive Daphne. When I listened to my storm playlist last night, I remember thinking I hoped it wasn't an omen that lightning would strike, and the pub would burn down. Only lightning *did* strike, but it struck me and not the pub. The *certain parts* of me that fancies Ryan aren't just in my abdomen anymore – they're in my chest, too.

If Ryan and Claudia are eloping, then it shouldn't take them long. Claudia's wedding with Arthur is supposed to happen this Saturday, and any eloping should happen before that, shouldn't it? Only with

Claudia, you don't really know. She would be reckless and selfish enough to leave Arthur standing by the altar waiting for her while she packs her suitcase for Las Vegas at a leisurely pace at home. Of course, she will have my mother pack it again afterwards to get it right. But I expect more from Ryan. Certainly, he understands the true meaning of an elopement. If he does, that leaves no more than six days where they both might be in town. I don't really care about Claudia being here, but I don't want to see Ryan ever again. So, I just have to stay indoors and drink and cry for a maximum of six days. I don't even have to get dressed for that. At the moment, it sounds very doable. Except for the crying part, it might actually be fun.

Ice cream doesn't work for me as comfort. As any other sane person working at a pub, I drink. Only today, I don't want to. I want to pretend I'm Claudia and wail like a three-year-old. I don't want ice cream, and I don't want to drink either. I do anyway because what else is there?

I grab my favourite whiskey in the kitchen cupboard. Fortunately, there are quite a few bottles because Gavin gave me a massive discount if I bought an entire case. I usually drink at the pub – it's practically a part of my job – and at the pub, it's on Gavin's tab. I prefer it that way. I truly love this whiskey, but today, I don't appreciate it the way I usually do. Suddenly, it tastes a bit sour, and the aftertaste is bitter. I know it's not – not this whiskey – but bitterness is all I taste. Bloody Ryan.

I'm more than halfway through the first bottle when there's a knocking on my front door. I've put on music, but it's not loud enough for anyone to rightfully complain about it.

"Go away," I snarl at the front door. More drinking, more knocking. I ignore it. But when the knocking turns into pounding, I get pissed. "Sod off," I roar. I'm drunk and in an awful mood, and the last time that happened, I punched Ryan, cracked his eyebrow, and broke his nose. It doesn't matter who's on the other side of the door. I'm not opening it – because they will get hurt.

"Open the door, Daphne." Ryan's voice sends a jolt of shock through my entire body. He's supposed to be eloping. He's not supposed to be here. And I don't want him here either – at least, I pretend I don't. But he keeps pounding on the door, and it's hitting a nerve, too – my non-existent patience.

"Piss off, or I'll break something else," I yell.

"Open the bloody door, Daphne," he roars. I don't know what he's doing here, but he should know better, and if he's here to gloat about his upcoming Las Vegas marriage, I'm going to kill him. Truly. Too bad for Ryan.

CHAPTER 16

Distress

Ryan

The cast makes an excellent door hammer, and it doesn't even hurt. Much. I don't care how long I have to stand here and how pissed the neighbours are going to be. I've been beaten, pushed into the harbour, bones have been broken, clothes ruined, and patience tested – so getting arrested does not discourage me at this point at all. I want to see Daphne, and nothing else matters to me. Yes, apparently, I'm *that* stupid.

When she finally opens the door, she tears it open with so much force I'm rather impressed it stays on the hinges.

"Go away," she sneers. If it wasn't Daphne I'm facing, I'd have thought she'd been crying. It immediately occurs to me that I don't like seeing her distressed like this. Not at all.

"No," I insist.

"I can't deal with all this fucking drama anymore," she yells – dramatically. "I've had it." She throws up her arms – dramatically – and retrieves into the flat. I take this as an invitation and close the door behind me before I go after her. She glances over her shoulder and frowns when she sees I've followed her.

The flat is nice. It's small and quite charming. The furniture is simple and timeless, but a few colourful pillows and posters spice up the look. On the grey couch, there's an ugly crocheted blanket with flowers and tassels. It looks cute and ridiculous at the same time. The window frames are painted dark blue, and one wall is beige. On the wall, there's a framed abstract poster that looks like a reproduction. It's mostly brown and vivid blue, but it has dashes of black and beige as well. At the bottom right corner, I see the signature – PM20 and a strange square. It seems familiar, but I have absolutely no idea where I might have seen it. All in all, the flat has soul and personality – just like its owner. The room has a faint smell of incense, and God help me, "Heat Wave" is playing softly on the stereo. Daphne punches stop on the remote so hard it's a wonder it doesn't break.

There's an almost empty bottle of Irishman, the Harvest, on the table, and Daphne grabs it and drains the rest of it. No wonder Myles was so hung over after the night he kept Daphne at the pub so I could meet Claudia at Luciano's. And no wonder you couldn't tell Daphne had been drinking at all. She wipes her nose indelicately with the back of her hand and glares at me. I hold out my hands in a calming gesture, but I don't think it'll work with her. She looks genuinely distressed. And rather pissed.

"Daphne …"

"No, I don't want to hear it." She waves me away, and despite the faint whiskey scent coming from her, her words aren't slurred, and her movements are perfectly controlled. If I hadn't seen the empty bottle, I would never have guessed how much she's probably been drinking.

"Listen ..."

"Pipe the fuck down, Ryan," she sneers. God, she looks angry. I may fear for my life, but I have to make her listen. She has to hear what I have to say.

"Daphne ..."

"No. No more. Marry Claudia and go far away. Find out if Rivendell is still standing. Just get the hell away from me. Both of you."

"Rivendell wasn't an option."

"Las Vegas then."

"We are not going to Las Vegas."

"Hawaii then. New Zealand, Grey Havens, Bahamas, wherever. I don't care. I don't want to know. I might even skip out on the required oh-and-ah ceremony Claudia will be hosting for the whole sodding town when the wedding pictures are framed." Daphne looks frustrated like she's already imagining what it will be like to be forced to fake the happiness Claudia will undoubtedly expect. Apparently, she agrees with her mother, my mother, and God knows how many else.

"I'm not marrying Claudia."

"Why not?"

"I can't."

"Pull yourself together, give the bloody notice, buy the ring, and wait the twenty-eight days. You don't even have to stay in town. Come to think of it, please don't!"

"That's not what I mean."

"What is it then?" she snaps.

"Unfortunately, I can't marry Claudia when I belong to someone else."

"Are you drunk too? And what the hell are you talking about?" she shouts angrily.

CHAPTER 17

Fury

Daphne

"Regretfully, I'm yours," Ryan says drily and rolls his eyes like he can hardly believe it himself.

"What?"

"This wasn't supposed to happen. You ruined everything," he says in a raised voice, like he's over the initial shock of the situation and suddenly remembers how pissed he is with me.

"Yes, do blame me for your own stupidity," I shout.

"For what? Choosing the bloody wrong sister in the first place?"

"What?"

"I chose wrong, Daphne. I don't know how the bloody hell I overlooked you for so long. How did I not see Claudia for what she was, and how did I not see _you_?"

"I avoided everything with a sweater vest," I point out. I don't mention I've always had my eyes locked on his ass every time he wore his jeans – sweater vest or not.

"I can't believe I feel this way about you after all you've put me through."

"Actually, I can't either," I say truthfully. It's a sobering thought. I wonder if he, at some point, hit his head so hard it has caused some serious damage. He's a gorgeous man, so why would he ever want *me?* Besides the obvious reason, of course. And he already got that.

"So," he says.

"So?"

"So, I'm yours. If you want me, that is …" He trails off, and for the first time ever, he seems unsure of himself. He probably is because, considering my behaviour, he might think I still hate him. I suppose I could have some fun with that, but you *don't* joke about winning the lottery. At least that's what it feels like when Ryan is standing here telling me he wants me. I've never been jealous of Claudia, not even the slightest, except the day she introduced Ryan as her boyfriend. I remember thinking he was all wrong for her but very right for me.

"Regretfully, I do."

"Am I going to survive it?" he asks tentatively.

"Depends."

"On what?"

"Are you going to kiss me?" He shakes his head and sighs deeply.

"If I must. Only to survive, of course."

"Of course."

We kissed last night at the pub, but this is something else. It's soft and caring, and apparently, we don't hate each other anymore. I never truly hated Ryan. I just hated the drama he brought. He might have hated me, and I don't even blame him. He doesn't kiss me like he hates me, though. He kisses me like he really likes me. Each stroke of his tongue is a caress, a soft touch, and a promise of pleasure. His stubble scratches my cheeks and chin and sends happy shivers up my spine. He has the cast and his hand on my hips, and I have my arm on his face and shoulder, and it feels … just right, honestly.

"No windscreen wiper," he mumbles.

"What?"

"I like kissing you," he says.

"Me too."

"That whiskey is really good."

"I have another bottle. It's my favourite." He looks me in the eyes, and there's definitely something there I haven't seen before. Not even when he was looking at Claudia, either. He takes my hand from his shoulder and kisses the palm. Then he looks at me seriously.

"Will you come with me?"

"Where?"

"Belgium."

"For how long?"

"About a year."

"Sure," I say and shrug. Ryan has a career. I work at a pub. It's not like I have something important going on. Particularly not after this Saturday when Claudia has moved in with Arthur and hopefully will leave my parents alone.

"You would?" he asks, clearly surprised. I wonder if I was not supposed to say yes. Or does he already regret what he asked?

"Well, yeah," I say because I mean it. "There are British pubs all over the world. I'll get a job. Can't be that hard with an authentic accent." Looking at him, I think I may be wrong. Maybe my accent isn't charming enough even abroad? Or maybe I'm just being naïve because he looks absolutely stunned. It's a look impulsive people get often enough. Believe me, I know.

"Um, we're not going to Belgium, Daphne."

"Why not?"

"Well, there are no present plans for another exchange."

"Were you testing me?"

"I suppose I was."

"You prick," I say and punch his chest. "Don't say that sort of thing if you don't mean it."

"So I gather."

"I want to go to Belgium," I pout. I've never been anywhere, and for a moment, I eyed the chance of seeing a tiny corner of the world outside call-the-bloody-puddle-whatever-you-want-town.

"Would you settle for a vacation?"

"Where are we going?" His eyes roam my body, and it's starting to feel hot in here.

"Somewhere where you will be wearing a bikini all day."

I'm wearing fucking pastels. Kill me now. I'm not even a bridesmaid – but I look like one. In bloody yellow pastels! Claudia is furious about … something. My mother thinks it's because Ryan chose me. My father thinks it's because she's finally, *finally,* moving out. My brother thinks it's because she's stuck with Arthur. I think it's because she didn't get her way. The seniors think it's because she's getting married – they don't recommend that. Ryan's parents and brother have their theories as well, but I'm fairly certain we'll never know them. They're very polite people.

I am, however, quite certain Claudia doesn't even know why she was furious when she told me I could no longer be a bridesmaid – like she demoted me. She also felt insulted when I didn't care at all. The only thing I cared about was the timing. Unfortunately, she told me this only ten minutes before the ceremony, so I had no time to run home and change. Our plumb cousin, with her curly red hair, pale skin, and blue eye shadow from her nose to her forehead, looks even worse than me, but somehow, she adores the dress, and she was so proud. Good for her, honestly.

I fidget in the pew. Something is itching at the back. Something is poking my ribs too. And don't get me started on the puff sleeves even Anne of Green Gables would be happy about.

"Love you in that dress," Ryan whispers.

"No, you don't," I snort because this dress … it's bloody awful.

"Yes."

"Why?"

"I've never shagged a bridesmaid," he says casually.

"I'm not a bridesmaid."

"Close enough."

"Cloakroom?"

"Cloakroom, bathroom, your old room, anywhere. Where is the reception anyway?"

"Promise?" I say and look up at him, bashing my eyelashes.

"Oh yeah, I fucking promise."

CHAPTER 18

Elation

Ryan

I suppose it shouldn't be a surprise even God herself didn't want to be present at Claudia's wedding. At least, that's what Daphne told me when we were in church right after she glanced at the ceiling to check if it was falling down because of all the dirty things I whispered in her ear during the ceremony. The hymnal has never been more useful, although I suspect neither the Oxford University Press nor Percy Dearmer imagined it would be used as a cover for an erection.

During these last few days, I must have touched Daphne a thousand times, and still, it's the only thing I want to do. We've spent an entire day naked in bed, talking, laughing, having out-of-this-world sex. At present, I am, of course, sporting a few bite marks. Now, it _is_ my concern, and I'm rather happy about that.

The wedding party is being held at Masterson's Function Rooms and Garden. Finally. Masterson is rather disappointed because every time Claudia called off a wedding with short notice, her parents had to pay a fifty percent fee – for nothing. I'm a bit disappointed, too, because I was looking forward to sneaking away and shagging Daphne in her old room. She's promised me we can play teenagers another day. Contrary to _my_ mother, Daphne's mother hasn't changed Daphne's room since she moved out.

Daphne has even hinted we could also shag in Claudia's room, which she's occupying until today after the wedding. I don't know what Claudia's room looks like – only what Daphne has briefly told me – and I seriously doubt a pink lace canopy with a round dome and a plastic chandelier can inspire anything but suicide. I'm honestly not certain I can even get it up – but then again, if Daphne gets on her knees in front of me … I'd better not think about that since I left the hymnal at church.

Claudia might be furious, but my mother is *elated*. Only that's probably not accurate enough to describe the immense joy she's feeling when she's looking at Daphne by my side, holding my hand. I haven't been home since the whole "let's go to Las Vegas" incident. I haven't told my mother where I've been, I've only texted her I was with a woman that was not Claudia and I'd see her at the wedding. She sent me a thumbs up and a laughing smiley. And then a peach and an eggplant. I'm certain that last one was courtesy of Myles who either hijacked my mother's phone or made up some kind of story as to why fruit and vegetable were required in that particular text. I consider letting Daphne lose on him later. That should be fun.

My mother hugs Daphne so fiercely I think I hear something cracking, but at least Daphne is still smiling, when my mother releases her.

"I'm thrilled, Daphne," she says seriously.

"Even if you might see Claudia once in a while?" Daphne enquires sweetly. *Too* sweetly, considering it's Daphne, we're talking about.

"Even then." My mother hesitates. "Not *too* often, though?"

As soon as my mother leaves us, Daphne pulls me towards the cloakroom.

"Come on, I want to show you something." I follow her gladly and watch as the sheer fabric of the modified dress curves around her ass. She ripped the fluffy underskirt from the dress the moment we arrived at the function rooms. The puffed sleeves went along with it, so she's now wearing a sleeveless, figure-hugging dress with a wide skirt. She looks like a sexy pin-up more than ever, and Gil Elvgren has painted a woman wearing a dress much like this. Ironically, the original is called "Too Much to Handle" – very fitting for Daphne. The bin by the cloakroom now looks like it spewed a fabric and haberdashery shop.

I let her drag me towards the bathroom, and a passing glance at the cloakroom bin confirms it hasn't been emptied yet. If Claudia sees this, the wedding festivities are probably going to end abruptly when the bride throws a fit. I think Daphne might be counting on it.

"Where are we going?" I ask when she pulls me inside the bathroom and towards one of the cubicles. She doesn't answer me but pulls me inside and closes the door. She smiles mischievously before she answers.

"I think you need to see how this dress looks from the back." She then turns in the narrow cubicle, and then she bends over, resting her hands on the cistern. When my mind registers what she's encouraging my hands are already opening my suit trousers.

"It looks dull," I claim, but it's obviously a lie. Daphne's ass would probably look spectacularly inviting in a cardboard box. Much like Marilyn Monroe did in the potato sack. Daphne looks over her shoulder – briefly at my hard cock – and then she starts pulling up the skirt until her ass is bare for me.

"How about now?"

"Much better." I almost growl. This time, I don't pull her knickers away – I rip them. And then I plunge once more. Only this time, there's no niggling doubt – not even a sliver.

Twenty minutes later, we return to the main room. Daphne stands in front of me and slowly runs her hands over my chest. She looks at me like she's pondering something.

"What is it?"

"Will you dance with my grandmother?"

"Sure," I say and shrug as I straighten my tie. For some reason, my answer makes Daphne squeal with joy and hug me. I didn't know she was this close to her grandmother.

"Remember to keep a straight face."

"Why wouldn't I?" I ask casually. If I can pretend to sing in church when I whispered dirty things to Daphne, then I sure as hell can pretend to Gladys, I've not just fucked her granddaughter in the bathroom.

As promised, I keep a straight face while dancing with Gladys, even when she pinches my ass. Contrary to Daphne, Glady's pinching isn't painful and contrary to Mrs Jeffreys, it isn't sexually suggestive either. If I had to guess, she probably just appreciates body parts that aren't as old and saggy as her husband's. I don't blame her, but I don't appreciate it either.

When I leave the dancefloor, I locate Daphne standing by a small alcove in the hallway with a heavy velvet curtain.

"I knew it," Daphne says delighted and pulls me behind the curtain. I have absolutely no idea what she's so happy about.

"Knew what? That she would pinch me?" Daphne snorts with laughter, and I don't understand how I've ever thought she was primitive. She is genuine and wonderful. And so beautiful.

"She pinched you?" she asks, and I nod because Grandmother Gladys did indeed pinch my ass. "It's your own fault, you know?"

"How can that possibly be my fault?"

"Looking so delicious."

"At least she didn't bite me."

"She has false teeth. She probably feared they'd get stuck in that firm ass."

"Well, you would know, wouldn't you?" Daphne smiles devilishly – she certainly still got it – and then she gets down on her knees in front of me. "You'd better not bite me *there*," I warn her.

"Don't worry, darling," she says only seconds before she sucks my cock into her mouth. My heart flutters at her words – and well, her mouth feels rather spectacular around my cock – but I feel elated thinking about being Daphne's darling. I want to be. I am. I know I am.

I've barely shoved my cock back in my pants, and Daphne has barely wiped her mouth when a woman approaches us. She must be someone from out of town because she oozes sophistication. She wears a royal blue off-the-shoulder dress, and of course, she wears pearls. I saw her looking at us earlier, but I didn't think much of it. Maybe she heard me in church, and maybe she knows exactly what Daphne was doing to me a few minutes ago. I was relatively quiet – at least, I think I was.

"Such a lovely couple," she says with a kind smile.

"Yes," Daphne says, smiling, but she's looking a little bit strained. "Claudia has been looking forward to this for a long time." I barely manage not to snort loudly. It would definitely have earned me an elbow in the stomach.

"Oh, not that elven-faced thing," the lady dismisses with a scoff. "I was talking about the two of you, my dear." Daphne looks stunned, and I feel a surge of satisfaction in my body. At least initially. Then I wonder how often Daphne has been dismissed as "the other sister" when people were fascinated with Claudia. I did, too, without even looking at her or considering who she was. What she was like. Daphne glances at me.

"He is quite pretty, isn't he?" she whispers conspiratorially, and the woman bursts out laughing. She looks me over – slowly – head to toe.

"That he is," she agrees. She winks at Daphne before she turns and leaves.

"*You're* beautiful, Daphne," I say quietly. She looks almost uncomfortable with the compliment. It's far from the first time I've told her that. Most of them might've been straight after sex, but of course, Daphne is beautiful even when she's not sporting a dazed post-sex look. "Truly." And it's not just because she had my cock in her mouth ten minutes ago.

"Really?" I nod, take her face between my hands and kiss her gently. In time, she'll know how beautiful I think she is. Everything about her. I think it might even top "secure another exchange abroad" on my to-do list for making Daphne happy.

And speaking of happiness, I don't think I've ever seen Daphne's parents this happy and at ease. They look peaceful, somehow, like a heavy burden has been lifted from their shoulders. Probably a blond burden. Both Gemma and John have easily accepted me as Daphne's boyfriend, and they even seem happy about it. And I don't think it's only because I didn't manage to disrupt Claudia's marriage to Arthur.

"You take care of our little girl," her father says.

"Yeah, right. You'd better ask her to take care of me."

"I'm sorry about the beetroot," Gemma says, and she looks quite contrite.

"That was the least of it," I snort. Because it really was.

Robert Collins approaches me, and at least it should be too early for him to have a chunk of food between his front teeth. Or not.

"Finally manned up, did you?" he says and claps my shoulder.

"Finally got my head out of my ass, you mean." Robert smiles.

"That's pretty common. A lot of people want the porcelain doll because it's pretty. But it's actually quite useless, isn't it?"

"Quite," I agree and laugh at the comparison. At the other end of the room, I spot Daphne standing on a chair. She's talking to Mr Dawson's teenage grandson, who's now the tallest man – if you can even call him that yet – in town. Oh, who am I kidding? She's scaring the piss out of him for gulping his grandfather's absinthe. The percentage of that one is not to be messed with, so I'll give the boy another minute or two until he keels over. He'll wake up tomorrow feeling shitty and only remembering being scolded – threatened – by Daphne. So, yeah, I think it's safe to say he won't be drinking for the next few years.

"I wouldn't want a porcelain doll either," Robert says with a look of longing towards Daphne. I can't blame him, but I still want to punch him.

"She surprised me," I admit. Robert smiles.

"Yeah, she does that." I remember him telling me this shortly after she broke my nose.

"I've got to say, you've got some balls on you, Ryan." He glances over my shoulder. "Definitely the tough brother," he says loudly with a smirk, and I have a feeling Myles has just passed by. I also know he probably winced at Robert's statement.

"Myles just went by?" I ask for confirmation. Robert grins delightedly and showcases a lump of something that looks like a mix of chips and dip between his front teeth.

"I wouldn't have the stones for it. Not many have." He looks slightly queasy.

"For what?"

"Daphne." He surprises me when he looks almost regretful. "Take care of her, alright?" I have a feeling my car will get flat on all four tires, too, if I don't. *At least* four flats.

"Why does everyone keep saying that?" I whine. "How about me?"

"Just do it," Robert says – and thank God his mouth is closed when he smiles this time.

"Yeah, well, if she one day shows up here with a Kilner containing a set of balls under her arm, you'll know I haven't."

CHAPTER 19

Love

Ryan

Next season

Daphne still hasn't forgiven me for not being stationed a year in Belgium. Or any other place for that matter. She appreciated the vacation, though. With her wearing a tiny bikini on Crete for two weeks, I was very happy, too. But there are still no immediate plans for me to be stationed abroad again, and she's not very happy about _that_. She's even talked to my boss about it each and every time they've met at company events. So far, he luckily finds her extremely charming, but I'm yet to tell him what she did to me last summer to get her way. Come to think of it, _she's_ the one who should be wearing those black wellies.

Since she last talked to my boss, she's found out the company has almost three hundred offices in more than thirty countries around the world. My boss is going to be in trouble the next time she sees him, and he'd better have his arguments in place. Urban planning is not a large part of the company portfolio but see if Daphne cares. I know she doesn't. My wife can be very persistent, and she holds grudges as well. Well, she's not my wife yet, but she will be someday soon if it's up to me. I've secretly been planning a beach wedding in Hawaii. It might be cliché, but Daphne will love it, and that's all that matters. And if I can persuade her to wear only a lei and a white bikini, then I'll be rather happy too.

We've been living together in Manchester for almost a year, and I quickly got used to having her here in my tiny flat. Daphne felt right at home, and Manchester has probably gotten used to Daphne, too, by now. Despite she's hardly ever been out of her small hometown her whole life she was undaunted at the prospect of living in a city with more than half a million people. The moment I dangled a key in front of her, she packed a bag and was ready to leave Puddle-whatever-town forever within ten minutes. Her parents left awfully quickly, too. Immediately after Claudia's wedding, they went on a three-month trip around the world where phone and internet connections were *extremely* bad. At least that's what they told Claudia. Daphne and I visited them in Dover. I extended the trip from Dover to Calais and then by train to Paris where we spent a few days. Daphne loved absolutely everything about it. I couldn't help thinking that Claudia would've had a fit of some sort if it'd been her on the train. Daphne is curious, excited, and grateful – and, most of all, happy. I'm grateful, too, and I'd take the broken bones of last summer any day to have her.

We've been saving money because Daphne wants to go to the Maldives. She wants to see the world now that she's finally "escaped" her childhood town. She stayed out of concern for her mother's health, and I can't help loving her a bit more because of it. Daphne can do anything she puts her mind to, but all she wanted was to take care of her mother. I must admit I'd break a few bones for Daphne's mother, too, by now. Her parents are truly wonderful people, particularly now they're free of the stress Claudia apparently caused.

We're back in Just-name-the-bloody-town for the summer season. Mostly, it's because of Daphne's parents, but also to uphold tradition. Besides, Daphne loves it here, and it's a cheap way to spend the summer with free room and board. The romantic guest room in my parent's house is ours, and with the noise Daphne and I often make when we have sex, I may finally get some revenge on my parents. Maybe I should even persuade Myles to stay here at least one night just for the fun of it.

On our first night back in town, we head for the pub.

"Do you think he still has the couch?" I ask with a smile and a wag of my eyebrows. Daphne lights up in a smile that never fails to make my heart pound faster. It makes something else pound, too, but I have to settle for a kiss, considering we're almost at the pub. A deep, long, thorough kiss.

"Most definitely. Unless it has decided to run off on its own, it was practically alive back then."

As we enter the pub, we're met with cheering and clapping.

"Hey, Daphne!"

"Welcome back to work," one even shouts optimistically. It's probably Gavin. People are genuinely happy to see her, and I feel so proud.

She ends up behind the bar, of course, because she thinks it's fun and because Gavin is as lazy as he's ever been. He's not lazy enough to skip complaining about how I've kidnapped his bartender/cooler/entertainment. There's nothing worse than listening to a grown man whine. Well, there is: listening to a drunk man whine because he has to work at his own place.

"Bravest man in town," a man calls out, and the cheering roars fill the pub. People raise their glasses, and several of them look at me with awe and respect. They're probably some of Daphne's previous victims. I accept the toast, and honestly, I relish it.

So, on our first night in town, Daphne ends up working at the old, dirty pub. We have local ale and the driest sandwich in history for dinner. No fuss, no parade like Claudia would have wanted. Thank God for that. Daphne likes simple things, and I'm starting to think she must be the lowest-maintenance woman in history. That's not why I love her, though.

*

Daphne's aunt's birthday is only a few days later. The Pitbull from last year comes running, and Daphne immediately gets on her knees to greet the happy creature. I must admit it's rather cute. Daphne really has a spectacular ass, and I find myself almost missing the red leather skirt she wore last year. A year ago, Arthur proposed to Claudia, and I was rather pissed about it. This year, I can't help feeling relief because I could've ended up making a colossal mistake.

"No ball this year, please."

"No need," Daphne says and discreetly grabs my balls. "I have what I need right here."

"No blue balls either."

"Like that would be my fault," she scoffs.

"You promised not to mention that," I whine.

"Then stop complaining." Truth is, we had a sex marathon a few weeks ago, and I must admit I'm the one who got sore. Well, Daphne was sore, too but she didn't complain about it as much as I did. And she wasn't the one who asked for a break – though she sure appreciated it. I also got blue balls after we argued, when she was working too much and even came home with a black eye. We hardly spoke – or did anything else – for two weeks. I ended up apologising and enrolling her in a Krav Maga class. I'm probably going to regret that one.

*

For some reason, the Kensingtons celebrate their marriage again this year. By now, I think we all show up merely to see how long they're going to pretend it's worth celebrating. Unfortunately, Mrs Jeffries hasn't died yet, so she's here again to make everyone uncomfortable. As soon as she sees me, she comes running, and only when she's standing almost in front of us does she notice Daphne.

"Daphne, my dear," Mrs Jeffries says quickly like Daphne was the real reason she came over.

"Mrs Jeffries." Daphne smiles, but I recognise the calculating look on Daphne's face – she's definitely considering if she should make some kind of trouble. And for once I completely support her way of thinking.

"Ah, and you brought Ryan, I see," Mrs Jeffries says politely. I'm certain she tries to be casual about her interest in me, but even I can see how eager she is. Besides, Daphne has seen just about every aspect of human nature working at pubs, and she easily recognises trouble in all shapes and sizes. She also *causes* trouble, of course.

"For *my* pleasure," Daphne emphasizes. God, I wish she'd chosen another word. Pleasure is not something you should encourage anywhere near Mrs Jeffries. And sure enough, she looks far too delighted for my comfort.

"We could share him," Mrs Jeffries suggests eagerly, but Daphne shakes her head.

"Not this one. He's *all* mine." Mrs Jeffries looks at Daphne with a frown on her face. Mrs Jeffries is used to women attempting to come to their boyfriend or husband's rescue, but so far, no one has been successful. Mrs Jeffries glares at Daphne. Daphne returns her glare. Mrs Jeffries keeps glaring in an attempt to stare Daphne down, but I know by now that Daphne never ever backs down when there's something she really wants. I'm arm candy again, but I certainly don't mind this time, and I stand completely still, and I even hold my breath, so I don't draw any attention to myself. After what seems like several minutes Mrs Jeffries sighs.

"All right, Daphne. All right." She glances regretfully at me and then turns on her heels and walks away. For the first time ever, I feel safe from Mrs Jeffries and it's all because of the fierce woman beside me.

"If I didn't love you before, then I certainly would now," I say in astonishment. "Last year, she suggested I walked around wearing only a collar."

"Did you?" she asks, grinning.

"For you, I would." That actually sounds very kinky and very appealing. Daphne must think so too, because she sends me a highly improper look. I feel it from the smile on my lips to the enthusiasm in my cock.

"We need to go shopping," she declares.

"I'm not buying a collar at Dalton's Barn!" I squeak. Dalton's Barn is the closest thing this nameless town has to a sex shop. He moved to town when his mother died, and going through her house, he discovered she apparently was a sex toy hoarder. Unsure what he should do about her extensive – unopened – collection, he started selling it. Discreetly at first, but after only a few weeks, he had a neon sign made and by now, it's locally as famous as the Las Vegas cowboy is globally.

So, Mr Dalton is now in the strange position of knowing everyone's sexual preferences and kinks, and honestly, he's not that good at keeping secrets. He has surprisingly many customers from the retirement home despite heart conditions, arthritis, and bad backs. Good for them, honestly.

"Please," Daphne begs.

"No," I insist. "Besides, there must be a larger selection back home."

"Do you have a preference?"

"If it means we're not getting me a collar from Dalton's barn, then yes, I have a preference. I want blue velvet and rhine stones," I claim as I try to come up with the most preposterous design imaginable.

Mrs Jeffries has decided not to challenge Daphne, not even when I'm on my own, because Mr Dalton has asked her to dance. I'm certain nothing good will come of it, and sure enough, when Daphne returns to me, she's almost keeling over with laughter.

"Mr Dalton says he has a velvet collar with rhine stones. It's a design sample he got for free. He's not certain about the leash, though."

"Leash?" I croak.

"Don't worry, darling," she says and pats my hand. "You're well-trained. We don't need the leash."

"I want the leash," I decide. I lean in and whisper in her ear. "Because I'm going to spank your ass if you even as much as mention Dalton's Barn again."

"Dalton's Barn," she says immediately. Well then, now I know what we're doing later. I should most certainly persuade Myles to stay over at my parent's house tonight.

*

It's bloody *boating* day. Daphne insists we should ask Mr Turner a ridiculous number of questions concerning his *boat* – simply to see if we can drive him mad enough to jump overboard. I rather like the idea. She's also wondering what she can say to make Arthur and Claudia join him. I rather like that idea, too. Daphne also insists we bring smaller bags. It's about half of what I would've bought, and I cross my fingers we won't encounter too much rain, waves, wind, or sunshine.

We've barely made it on to the jetty where The Princess is anchored when I feel a forceful bump to my side. This year, at least, I manage to close my mouth as I plunge into the dirty water in the marina. This year's summer is no better than last year's, so the water is freezing. Of course, it is. When I surface, I see Daphne in the water, too, swimming alongside me.

"What the hell, Daphne?"

"Oh no," she says – dramatically. "Clumsy me. We're all wet. We can't go on the boat like that." And that's when I'm certain I really, truly love her. I don't care about getting wet, but I certainly care about not spending an entire day on Mr Turner's *boat*. My father glares at her, and for a moment, it almost looks like he's about to jump in and join us. I've heard from my parents and Myles that last year's trip was a disaster. There are only so many hours you can listen to a man talk about himself, and unfortunately, out to sea, there's nowhere to run. He probably does it on purpose.

Myles holds out a hand to help me out of the water, which is very unlike him.

"Pull me in," he whispers desperately. I'm not doing him any favours, and thanks to the much smaller bag, I can crawl onto the jetty on my own. Daphne's father has helped Daphne out of the water, and he looks crestfallen. Probably because Daphne is the only entertaining thing here today, and now she's not going sailing with him. Gemma has been clever enough to fake illness and is at home on the couch, probably eating biscuits and drinking tea.

"Come on, I'm freezing," Daphne says loudly and starts walking quickly away from The Princess.

"Where are we going?"

"Dry clothes and a better boat are waiting for us at the other end of the marina."

We run across the marina to the *sunny* side. Daphne stops at a truly beautiful boat with a dark blue hull and mostly everything else is teak. I'm surprised to see Mark, the DJ, onboard. Surprised and happy.

"It's only thirty-three feet. Do you think you can manage?" he says when he sees my surprise.

"Hell yeah, I'll manage," I say as I accept the hand he offers me. Daphne is already onboard and rummaging through a monstrous bag for dry clothes. She hands me a large, fluffy towel.

"Nice escape," Mark says, grinning at Daphne. "I could hear the splash all the way here."

"Do you sail the boat on your own?" I ask as I dry off.

"Of course I do," he scoffs. "Do you think I'm Mr Turner?"

Out at sea, Mark handles the boat like a pro, and when the wind picks up, Mark and "The Blue Pearl" show us what they can really do. I can't help but being impressed. Daphne is, of course, cheering loudly at the speed.

"Wow, Mark. This is fast," I say, smiling because this is really fun. I've never had a sailing experience like this. The boat cuts effortlessly through the water, and it's a smooth, beautiful ride. Mark grins, delighted.

"Nigh uncatchable and the only ship that can outrun the Dutchman." We fly past The Princess like a Formula 1 racer passes a Kia Forte driven by an old woman. I catch a glimpse of Myles and my parents, who look like they're about to jump ship. Probably because Mr Turner is still on board.

*

Daphne persuades me to go to the senior's market day. It wasn't that difficult, really, because she promised she'd make it up to me. Every minute I'm there will earn me a minute's reward when we get back. Come to think of it, I should have brought a tent.

"Why do you even want to go?" I ask.

"To see is everyone is still alive. And I want to buy the ugliest thing there and give it to Claudia."

"Too late. I bought the ugliest things last year. I think it was a mouse."

"Mr Dawson made those."

"Really?"

"He had actually hoped he could use it to scare his daughter at Christmas."

"Well, it sort of worked. Myles screamed." He truly did. When he started opening the gift-wrapped mousy thingy I'd gotten him, he looked very suspicious – as he should. He wasn't prepared for the content, though and let out a very girly shriek when he saw it.

At the field where they've set up market day, I'm received like a soldier returning home from battle. They remember my heroic effort last year when I chased Mrs Cross' nephew Neil off, but mostly, they remember my heroic effort to man the booths while they were having a good time, gossiping, and drinking tea. I have no doubt they appreciated that more.

"Well, at least you haven't enrolled me all day this year," I say with a pointed look at Daphne, which she completely ignores. She still hasn't admitted she's the one who volunteered me last year.

"This year, I've come up with something better," she says with a smile. At the knitting booth, I see Mr Dawson's grandchild. When he sees Daphne, he flinches slightly and though I feel sorry for him, I can't help laughing. The read-haired boy from last year, who wanted Daphne to be his aunt, is here this year too, and he looks shocked to see me holding her hand. When I kiss her, too, he gives me an evil eye, and I feel so much better. *This year,* it might very well be the best day of summer.

*

Five minutes after we arrive at the Pink Party, Daphne has secured her own bottle of rosé and put a straw in it. One sip, and she's drained almost half of it, and I'm starting to think that's the way to get through this day. Only I don't like rosé. I like beer, but hell no, if I'm drinking that fruity shit some of the men here have settled for. That's not how beer is supposed to taste like. And raspberry has no business in gin either, for that matter. Myles demonstrates this by almost spitting out the drink he's just taken a sip off – just like a child who's gotten his first taste of broccoli. He reluctantly swallows, and then he discreetly dumps the content into a salad bowl with something undeterminable pink in it. The gin might actually make it taste better. Clearly, it's going to be a very, very long day for me. Maybe I can convince Daphne to "accidentally" spill something on me. Again.

*

As we arrive at the Percival residence, Daphne cracks her knuckles. It's Stephen's sixth birthday, and as it turns out, I'm not the only one who thinks he's a twat. We quickly discover that the evil yellow car still lives, only this year, its status as a favourite is replaced with a blue, larger one. When it heads towards my foot, I take a page from Daphne's book of accidents and "unfortunately" step on it.

"Oh, so sorry," I lie quickly, and Mr Percival sends me a sympathetic smile. He knows perfectly well what I did, and apparently, he doesn't blame me one bit – maybe that's even how he deals with it. At least Stephen doesn't start screaming – not even at the crunching sound the car makes – because his younger brother Alistair chooses that moment to come within an arm's reach. He promptly gets rammed. He doesn't cry, so I assume he's gotten used to the blue car by now. I also recognise who will be the wimpy brother of the two. And it's not going to be Alistair.

"Is that how you and Myles started out?" Daphne asks like she's just read my mind.

"Well, to be fair. Myles was never evil."

"Good thing. Wimpy and evil are a horrible mix," she says and glances towards Stephen with a frown. She then pinches her eyes, and whatever she's thinking can't be good.

"Devilish and tough isn't much better," I claim. "Just look what happened to me last season." Daphne looks at me and smiles.

"Then you'd better stand back."

Daphne locates the degraded yellow car and snatches it off the couch. She then discreetly nudges Stephen when he's standing next to the family dog. He turns instantly, drops the car, and then lunges at the dog with a shriek. The dog is an Old English Sheepdog turned Greyhound from living with Stephen, and it escapes him easily. Daphne grabs the blue car and takes my hand. I can hardly keep a straight face when we casually wander out to the back garden. To everyone, we must look like a couple in love looking for some quiet time alone. She steers us straight to the koi pond, where she kicks loose a few stones from the edge. She shoves one stone into each car and then promptly dumps them into the deep end of the pond. And just in time, because Alistair comes running across the lawn along with the sheepdog. It's wagging its tail and is not missing any patches of fur, so I'm certain it got away from Stephen safely.

"Daphne, Daphne, Daphne," Alistair cheers again and again as he rushes closer. When he's almost close enough he lunges for her, and Daphne barely manages to catch him. She swings him, and he screams with joy. Incidentally, the koi pond is far from the house where the birthday twat is now screaming, too – probably because he can't find his murderous blue car. Too bad we can hardly hear him.

I pet the dog while Daphne has kicked off her shoes and is running around playing with Alistair. He's blond and blue-eyed and is just about the cutest child in town. Like any … well, *most* other children, he's taken an instant liking to Daphne. She's going to be a wonderful mother someday.

*

At this year's softball tournament, I'm in the red team. Daphne is too, and just like last year, she's out for blood. Only this year it's fortunately not mine. When Daphne isn't focused on hitting me like she was last year, she's an astonishing player. Not only does she hit home runs like there's no other way to hit, but she also pitches and catches like a pro. Daphne's father is seriously considering if he should have a cup of tea in the middle of the field while Daphne's playing ball. She hardly needs the rest of us to completely wipe out the other team in the first round.

Claudia is sniffing the glove, Myles is still useless, and Arthur keeps mumbling something about, "There certainly must be town rules against this because it is hardly fair." Their massive defeat will go down in town history, I'm certain. We – well, honestly mostly Daphne – end up winning the tournament.

CHAPTER 20

Astonishment

Daphne

"So, it's true?" Ryan asks.

"What is?" I've been humming "I Kissed a Girl" while we're walking to Leslie and Christina's wedding at Leslie's parents' function room. I have some very good memories from last year – Ryan probably doesn't.

"That Christina has kissed you?" I smile and nod because it's true. "Did you kiss her back?" Ryan asks, and he looks awfully interested.

"Only because I was tipsy and thought she was Michael Sanders."

"How on earth can you mistake the two of them?"

"He pretty much looked like a girl until he turned seventeen." Ryan widens his eyes in surprise. Michael Sanders now rides the largest motorbike in town. Except his face he's got tattoos all over – yes, I do mean _all_ over, but I'm not telling Ryan that particular detail – and he almost looks like a blonde, bearded version of Dwayne Johnson.

"Did you have a thing for Michael?"

"Absolutely."

"For how long?"

"Until last summer," I say. Grabbing the lapels of Ryan's suit jacket, I kiss him. So far, Ryan hasn't been jealous, but let's face it, with Michael there's *a lot* to be envious about, and not only his six-foot-five height.

"Did you just close that subject," he wonders when he lets go of me.

"Do you want to talk about Michael and his ..." Ryan holds up his hand.

"No," he snaps. "I prefer to pause my brain on the fact that you could mistake him for Christina until he turned seventeen."

"You're going to give him shit about it the next time you see him, aren't you?"

"Absolutely," Ryan says with a grin.

When we arrive at Leslie's parents' house, I can't help but stop and stare. I know I'm not considered a romantic girl, and usually I'm not, but this is so beautiful. On each side of the long gravel drive, they've set out garden torches. The torches don't give much light, but it's enough to see the flower decorations on the ground and the bows of white veils on the poles that show the way to the party. It's twilight, the dew is starting to fall, and I hear bats flapping about. Leslie and Christina were married this afternoon. Their family and closest friends were here for dinner, and the rest of town is invited for the fun part – the party.

Ryan gets side-tracked by Mark almost the moment we've made it down the stairs, but I don't mind. I've been away from town for most of the year, and there are so many people I want to see and talk to. But unfortunately, Claudia locates me first. She looks bored, and she just watches me with a vacant expression until I feel compelled to say something. I might as well get it over with, or I'll risk her following me around all night.

"So, how's married life?" I ask. Not that I care.

"Alright, I suppose."

"And Arthur?"

"He's awfully hairy," Claudia says with a displeased frown. I can't say I'm surprised, and I'm about to suggest she buys a shearing machine when she says: "Thank God sex only takes a few minutes." I did *not* need to know that. "He expects me to keep house." Claudia looks nonplussed, like it's the strangest thing she's ever heard.

"So?"

"What do you mean 'so'?"

"It's not like you're working."

"Don't be ridiculous, Daphne. He also expects dinner when he gets home."

"So?" I know for a fact that Claudia can barely open the refrigerator without help.

"I don't cook," she says in disgust.

"Then make a deal with Halil. Get him to deliver dinner every night."

"I don't like Luciano's."

"Why not?"

"Their Riesling tastes funny."

"What does Riesling taste like?

"Nice."

"What's that like?"

"Like wine." I look at her, and I must admit I haven't missed her at all. I didn't imagine I would, but it would've been nice to have been mistaken. She is my sister, after all. The voice of the Ed Sullivan character from Pulp Fiction suddenly rings out:

"Ladies and gentlemen, now's the moment you've all been waiting for. The world-famous Jack Rabbit Slim's Twist Contest. Now this is where one lucky couple will win this handsome trophy that Marilyn here is holding. Now, who will be our first contestants?" I squeal happily, and Claudia dramatically claps her hands over her head. I turn around, already kicking off my shoes. "Alright, now let's see what you can do. Take it away." Ryan is already on the dance floor without his shoes. He's holding out his hand in invitation, and I make it to him only seconds before the "You Never Can Tell" starts. Normally, I would say that "Heat Wave" is *our* song, but this might actually be it. I fancied Ryan, but I think I fell in love with him last year when we were dancing to this.

"Go, Uma," someone shouts, making me laugh. It's probably the same drunk person as last year.

When we've finished our version of the "Pulp Fiction"-twist, Ryan keeps me on the dancefloor. We sway slowly to "Lonesome

Town" – also from "Pulp Fiction". I love this song, it's beautiful and sad and one of those songs you feel to the pit of your stomach. I lay my head on Ryan's shoulder, close my eyes, and just enjoy the moment.

"You truly never can tell, Daphne," Ryan says quietly.

"What are you talking about?" I say and lift my head so I can look at him.

"Well, last year, I never could tell what you were going to do. Or how much it was going to hurt," he says with a pointed glare. I should probably feel guilty – I did at the time – but everything I did to Ryan last year has led to us being together. And hell no, if I regret that. I only feel fortunate I didn't execute my plan with the shovel. It's the perfect tool, really. You can hit someone with it and then dig a hole for their dead body.

"I'm not sorry," I tell him.

"I know. I'm not either. At the time, I couldn't tell how much I'd grow to love you either." He pauses. "But I do." He pulls away from me, gets down on one knee and holds out a ring. "Will you marry me?" Suddenly, there's awfully quiet in the room; everybody is watching us, and I can't help thinking they're not supposed to do that. It's not our party – it's Christina and Leslie's. I'll be the first to admit I'm not often rendered speechless, but right now? I want to scream yes from the top of my lungs, but instead, my eyes start watering. My lower lip is quivering, and my throat is burning. I'm completely overwhelmed and happier than I've ever been. I can hardly believe this is happening to me. Since I apparently can't answer him, I just snatch the ring from Ryan and put it on.

"That's a yes," Myles roars delighted nearby. The guests cheer as Ryan gets up. And when he kisses me, you might think England has *finally* won the World Cup again. Christina and Leslie come rushing to us in their identical dresses. Christina hugs me fiercely and squeals delightedly.

"I'm so happy for you." She hugs me again and turns towards Ryan. "You are marrying the town's best kisser, Ryan." Christina declares. Leslie clears her throat.

"Second best," she corrects Christina with a smile before she hugs me.

"Second best," Christina agrees when they're both done crushing my bones. They look so happy, and I feel just like them – wonderful, happy, in love.

My parents finally make their way through the crowd of well-wishers. I feel a bit guilty about being the centre of attention at Christina and Leslie's wedding, but they both assure me they love it. Besides, Ryan asked them if it would be alright if he asked me to marry him today. Turns out he fell in love with me to "Never Can Tell," too. Well almost. At least until I stepped on his toes, and he broke his arm. That certainly put a damper on his enthusiasm.

"I love you," my father says and holds me close. When he's not stressed because of Claudia, my dad is a very emotional man, and I'm not surprised to feel his body quivering slightly. "I'm so happy," he whispers, and I can hear in his voice how heartfelt it is. My parents have always taken care of me – and I've taken care of them too. Claudia is oblivious, Gary is delusional, and my parents and I have often felt like the only normal people in the house.

I hug my mother, and when I turn towards Ryan again, he hands me an envelope.

"What's that?"

"It's from my parents."

"What is it?"

"Tickets."

"For what?"

"Our wedding." I frown, but I can't fail to notice how excited Ryan is – despite he's doing his best to hide it. When I open the envelope, I find a printout of tickets from Heathrow to … Honolulu.

"We're getting married in Hawaii?" If that's the case, then I'm going to have the most indecent wedding photos ever because I won't be putting on many clothes.

"We are. If you want to? Just the two of us."

"Oooh," my mother says and claps her hands happily. She looks so thrilled despite the fact she'll miss my wedding, and it puts me at ease immediately. She's always wanted me to do whatever made me happy – regardless of her own desires. She and my father have suggested several times that I leave town, even if it meant they were the only ones left to deal with Claudia. Only I couldn't do that to them.

"You're joking. Of course I will," I squeal and jump into Ryan's arms. I might also wrap my legs around his waist because my dress has a wide skirt – for obvious reasons – and because my future husband is sexy like hell.

"Looks like Daphne accepted the wedding location," Myles says from behind me. Damn it! I reluctantly let go of Ryan and judging by the bulge in his trousers, he's not happy about Myles' interruption either. I turn and see Myles, along with his parents. I love these people – and not only because of the plane tickets. I hug them happily and gratefully. But right now, I'd like nothing better than to pull Ryan to the bathroom and have my way with him again.

"What's going on?" someone from the back of the crowd yells.

"We're getting married in Hawaii. On the beach," I yell back. I have absolutely no idea who's asking. There's a mix of cheers and awe. I think it's by far the most exotic thing to ever happen for anyone here. I'm not even certain all of them know where Hawaii is, but they know it's far more exotic than this place.

"I don't like it, there's sand on the beach," Claudia complains like she's invited. She's not.

"Now, love, there's something important we need to talk about," Ryan says seriously.

"What is it?"

"How few clothes are you going to wear?"

"Ugh, I'm not listening to this," Myles complains, tortured as he stalks off.

"You'll have to wait and see," I say with a smile. Truth is, I already know what I want to wear. I want a white bikini and a long sheer sarong. I want a Frangipani behind my ear and a necklace made from seashells. I want to get married in the evening and have torches like Leslie and Christian have today. And if I have any say in it, I want Ryan barefoot in casual, white linen trousers and shirt. I have no idea how he feels about a seashell necklace or bracelet, but I'm going to find out.

The Emotional Rollercoaster

Daphne

October

Sunday morning doesn't get much better than this. I'm in the armchair with my tablet in the living room of our flat in Manchester, and my feet are propped up on Ryan's lap. He's reading on the couch, and he absentminded strokes my ankle and shin. His hair is standing in all directions, and he looks like he just rolled out of bed after having hot morning sex. And that's rather accurately how the morning started. Now somewhat dressed, he's wearing a pyjama bottom and a white tank top and looks absolutely delectable.

I'm wearing a white cotton nightdress with straps and a scalloped hem Ryan got me. He loves it. And he loves even more that the size of my tits and ass make it look rather indecent. A larger size would've been better – at least if you were going for the fit. Apparently, Ryan wasn't.

Our wedding photo is the background of my tablet and I find myself looking at it often. I can't help smiling each and every time I see it. I got it just the way I wanted. Ryan refused a shell necklace but liked the shell bracelet. He also got a Hawaiian hook necklace made of bone and with a leather strap. I like the necklace, Ryan does too, but what he really loves is to tell people that he got it for our wedding, because he got me hooked and reeled me in. Intelligent people can be very stupid sometimes.

I put down the tablet and poke him with my foot.

"Hmm, what is it love?" Ryan glances briefly at me. He's reading some masterplan about holistic city planning and he's completely absorbed in it. I don't mind, really, but sometimes I just get restless. Particularly when I'm keeping a secret – I'm so bad at it.

I'm very proud of Ryan. I think he's clever, dedicated, and ambitious, but not so much that it becomes unbearable. He's not self-important either, and that's why I don't mind he's working Sunday morning. Sometimes, I still can't believe he loves me and married me – in Hawaii, no less. The paperwork is still underway, but we said, "I do", so it counts! It's difficult to believe I'm his wife and it's equally difficult to accept he's proud of me too. When I first got to Manchester, it was mostly because I kicked hooligans out of the pub I worked in. Now, it's because I'm doing well at a family centre as a family support worker.

My boss at the family centre is called Chiaki, and she's a tiny, fierce woman of Japanese descent. She's covered in Irezumi tattoos, and nobody seems to know whether she really has ties to the Yakuza or if she just likes the design. She likes to keep people guessing. I think it's hilarious, and ever since the first time I saw her send a particular nasty ex-husband's lawyer packing, I went with the Yakuza connection. She's *not* thrilled – particularly not because I interject, "This is what you get for fucking around with Yakuzas!" every chance I get. Obviously, she does not appreciate "Kill Bill" the way she should, and she does *not* like to be compared to Gogo Yabari.

Chiaki is a tough woman with a big heart and she's worried about me too – or rather worried I'm so impulsive. Now, where have I heard that before? She thinks I might be a tad too dedicated too, and Ryan enrolled me in a Krav Maga class the first time I got home with a black eye because I got in the middle of something I shouldn't. I don't regret it, though, because the alternative was to stand by and watch a man punch his tiny wife and drag her away by the hair. Chiaki was *not* amused – neither about the situation, the black eye, the Krav Maga, or talking to the police afterwards – and she has made me promise I'll never again kick a man *after* I've taken him down. Even if he is another child-abusing, wife-beating bastard who deserves it. I may have crossed my fingers when I made that promise.

Despite the whole "don't bloody kick another bastard incident," Chiaki wants me to get a proper education, and she also wants me to keep working at the family centre. I'm very grateful and I know I'm going to, but there's something more important happening first. Something I'm about to tell Ryan.

"So, I'm going on a rollercoaster ride," I say casually. Ryan snorts and glances at the ceiling.

"Yeah? Would that be Formula Rossa in Abu Dhabi or The Kingda Ka in New Jersey?" During the past year Ryan has learned every time I want to do something – anything really – I want it to happen in another country simply because I want to travel. Except for Crete and Hawaii, it's been short trips and extended weekends, but we've seen a lot of Europe's capitals by now. And why the hell Claudia didn't want to go to Copenhagen, I'll never understand.

"No, something more local," I tell him.

"Really?" I have his complete attention now because this is *very* unlike me. "We don't have any big rollercoasters in Manchester, Daphne," he says. When I nod, he frowns. "Not unless you've persuaded someone to build one?"

"No, it's more like an emotional rollercoaster."

"Oh God," Ryan moans. "Don't tell me you've invited Claudia!" I start laughing at this because that's never going to happen.

"No."

"What is it then?"

"More oestrogen than usual."

"More what?" I've clearly lost my clever hus … oh, apparently not. "You're pregnant?" He sits up straight and bumps a knee against the coffee table, making everything clatter. The master plan flows to the floor as he looks at me. I nod, and I can feel myself tearing up. Ryan almost looks teary, too, and I burst out crying with an indelicate snort. I've never been the elegant type. He immediately hugs me and holds me close. He kisses my hair, and I can feel he's smiling. When I raise my head to look at him, it only confirms it.

"So, I take it now's not a good time to tell you there might be an opportunity to go to Amsterdam for half a year?" he asks with a smile and slight shake of his head.

"When?"

"Probably two months' time."

"We're going," I say immediately.

"Are you sure?"

"I have maternity leave. They have hospitals in the Netherlands, too."

"I have to clear it with my boss."

"Let me talk to him." There's *no way* Ryan's boss is preventing me from going to Amsterdam, and I try very hard not to make it sound like a threat, and I'm certain I can buy a shovel in Manchester too. Ryan frowns – apparently, he sees straight through me.

"Let's keep that as a last resort. Okay, love?" He gently caresses my stomach. "How far along are you?"

"Nine weeks." I can almost see the wheels turning in his head as he makes the calculation.

"*Please* tell me it was the night Myles stayed over at my parent's house." He grins and looks truly excited about that possibility.

"Could be."

"It definitely is. I just decided."

"Do you think that'll make your parents forgive you?"

"With a grandchild, they'll forgive me anything," he claims.

"I can't wait to tell Claudia."

"Why?"

"She'll stay far away from us forever when faced with a baby."

"She doesn't like children?"

"Are you joking? The smell, they drool, they can't eat properly, they're dirty, and they claim all the attention she thinks is meant for her."

Arthur and Claudia are still married. So far, at least. Arthur has turned out to be bisexual, with a *clear* preference for men. He never did care much about kissing Claudia – or doing much of anything else with her for long, for that matter. But she made the perfect front for his ultra-conservative family. A beautiful but utterly useless woman you just have to love in order to be able to stand her for more than five minutes. At least, that's what people thought. Only he doesn't care about her much. He does, however, care very much about a flamboyant twink from Birmingham called "Glam," who's into K-pop and lots and lots of glitter. He also has an interest in "home movies" and "artistic photography". Arthur wants to marry him; his parents say absolutely not, but so far, Arthur is defiant and determined. Nobody knows how Glam feels about all of this.

Claudia is stunned. Or oblivious. I don't quite know which. She still doesn't understand why she has to either work or keep house. She hasn't asked for a divorce, and she doesn't seem upset about either Glam or her husband's preferences. She's only wondering if she can keep living in the house, and if anything, concerning the situation merits, she gets a housekeeper to take care of everything. Not for the first time I wonder what she does all day.

My parents had her IQ tested because it suddenly occurred to us that if she didn't understand what was going on, that might be the reason she didn't care about what was happening. We all felt very guilty about not considering that earlier until she scored 95 on the test. That means her intelligence is not the reason she's acting like she is. They also put her through plenty of psychological tests – she truly loved those, of course – but none of them indicated there was something wrong with her besides being utterly selfish. And that's not a medically accepted diagnosis. They considered Alexithymia – also called emotional blindness – at some point, but the only symptom she has is indifference to other people. She was very disappointed she didn't get a diagnosis. My conclusion on Claudia's many tests? She's got her head so far up her own ass it must be painful. I also admire the acrobatic skills it must take to pull it off.

On other local Puddle-without-name-town news, I can report the following:

For the remainder of the season, Ryan teased Michael Sanders relentlessly about looking like a girl until he turned seventeen. Michael got rather tired of that and thought Ryan should break a few bones this season as well, and he'd be just the right man for the job. They met over a pint in the pub – which I served – and compromised. Ryan promised he would stop teasing him if Michael promised to stop looking at me with a filthy smile like he knows what I look like naked – he does. Michael promised to stop thinking about me naked if Ryan stopped reminding Michael which one of them I was about to marry in Hawaii, wearing very little clothes. Which Michael, by the way, wasn't allowed to think about due to their compromise.

Mr Kensington was caught high as a kite on Viagra fucking Mrs Jeffries in the middle of the park. They were both arrested for public indecency, and the arresting officers were recommended to contact a crisis hotline immediately! Apparently, it had been quite the show. The playground equipment they used was torn down the very moment local police removed the barricade tape.

Mrs Cross fortunately still lives, but her nephew Neil has died in a traffic accident. Ironically it involved a horse trailer that was on its way to pick up Artax, who had just won the derby and cost Neil an awful lot of money he didn't have. Now, *that* story has finally ended.

In greater news, the seniors in town have agreed on a name: "Town-upon-Puddle" – or on rainy days "Puddle-upon-Town" – like it's an important place like Stratford-upon-Avon. Sadly, it's the best suggestion they ever come up with. They've already made T-shirts and Mr Dawson has purchased the website domain – both of them. I wonder what he's going to do with them. So far, the T-shirt only has the town name(s) on it, but I hear arguments about which landmark they're going to put on the next round of shirts have already started. I didn't even know we had landmarks in town, and I don't think the abandoned Kensington-BMW counts.

Luciano's – the most romantic place in town – is still there, still serving *Riesling*. Claudia still sends it back at least once every time she's there, and Halil gladly changes glasses until she stops complaining. It's the same Riesling he's served for years because it's his wife's favourite. Halil still pretends to be Italian, and he still doesn't speak a word of it. "Grazie mille" still sounds like "brazen milf". Mrs Jeffries loves that, of course.

My parents are thriving. My mother is happy, and I think my father is relieved they managed to marry Claudia off. They don't see her that often and frequently pretend they're out of town. Gary is still self-important and still without reason.

Ryan's parents went through just about any emotion when Ryan told them about the pregnancy. Surprise, forgiveness – you know, with the noise and all – happiness, and protectiveness. I've got to say I now completely understand why Ryan and Myles refer to their mother as "The Colonel" when she doesn't hear them. When she had finished telling me how, now that I was pregnant, I was *done* taking any risks concerning my job, or because of my temperament and impulsive nature, I could only squeak:

"Yes, ma'am."

Myles is looking forward to becoming an uncle and threatened to corrupt *Ryan's* child any way he could until I reminded him it was *my* child, too. He retracted his threat, and he then started laughing because apparently that the baby is *my* child is worse for Ryan than anything Myles has to offer. He's definitely still the wimpy brother. Both Ryan and I remind him often.

Now, two months after the residents of Town-upon-Puddle first time heard of Glam from Birmingham, Arthur is still married to Claudia. He's also a reluctant internet porn star and calendar model. And I know things about Arthur I truly wish I could unsee and unhear. He's even hairier than I imagined – all over! He has the worst duckface pout in the world – not that duckface has ever done anyone any good besides the bird. It doesn't get any better when he's ass up and wearing a barely-there elf costume for the December photo of the calendar. (Arthur and this particular costume also featured in the movie "Santa's Favourite Candy Cane".) He has a decent-sized cock, but it still looks ridiculous when he's wearing a costume or covered in glitter. And he sounds like a chicken when he orgasms.

And then there's Ryan … Ryan has promised both mine and his parents that we'll visit often before we go to Amsterdam. Yes, we're going! – and I didn't even have to talk to his boss. He's also promised we'll visit often when we return home. Who knows, in time, he might even grow to like the town, despite the fact I got him a collar from

Dalton's Barn … No, seriously, I didn't. He does spank me once in a while, though, and I don't mind one bit.

Ryan is everything to me. He's the love of my life, but he's also the prick I punch in a hormonal fury when he leaves the seat up, and I almost fall into the toilet bowl when I go to the bathroom during the night. He's also the idiot who snores very loudly when he's drunk, and I just have to wake him up with an elbow to his ribs. At least he hasn't broken anything since last summer.

*

We're leaving in ten minutes, and I've only just finished packing my suitcase for Amsterdam when Ryan comes into the bedroom. He finished packing yesterday because he's just that kind of a go-getter. He prefers to call it "proactive", but he's really just an eager beaver. Wanker.

We've already sent a few things ahead, but not much. We're only staying six months and I'll shop for the baby when we get there. I don't know much about Dutch stores for either furniture or babies, but they have an IKEA, so I don't think they can be entirely uncivilized. Ryan snorted at this because he doesn't think having an IKEA anywhere *near* your home is something to aspire to. Nor does he think IKEA in any way contributes to civilization. I can spend an entire day there, but that's probably because I've lived in the same stupid little town my entire life. Normal people probably wouldn't do that.

"Ready, love?" Ryan asks.

"Depends."

"On what?"

"Still regret you're mine?"

"What?"

"That's what you told me when you knocked on my door. 'Regretfully, I'm yours'." Ryan laughs and nods as he remembers.

"I don't regret it. And I've survived so far, haven't I?" he says, and he looks rather proud of the achievement.

"Only because you kissed me."

"Then I'd better kiss you again, so I make it to the airport." He kisses me, and I can't say I'm going to complain if he fears for his life, and this is the consequence. "I'm not going to ask you if you regret anything," he says. "I know you don't. Not even breaking my bones."

"The nose suits you. You look tough." Ryan's nose has the slightest bump since it's been broken, and I'm not lying when I say it suits him. He runs his fingers over it.

"Agreed. But I tell people I broke it in a bar fight."

"That's not entirely untrue," I agree because he was in the pub when I punched him. Only there wasn't much of a fight.

"I make it sound more dramatic than it was. I tell everyone I was fighting a man and that I got a few punches in. Of course, I won."

"Of course you did, darling," I say sympathetically. "I did feel a bit guilty at some point," I admit.

"Really?" When I nod, Ryan looks astonished. "Wow, I'm almost disappointed."

"Was I that bad?"

"You are a hellish creature," he says. But at least he kisses me again.

"Well, at least you knew what you were getting into when you married me."

"True." He kisses me gently before he looks at me seriously. "Now tell me what you promised my mother."

"No working in pubs."

"And?"

"Bars or anything even remotely like it."

"And?" I groan, exasperated because we've been over this a million times. At least! I honestly think that Ryan is behind it. His mother, Bridget, was merely the tool he wielded to make me agree. And she was more than happy to comply. I didn't suspect a thing when she said she had a day off and would love to take her daughter-in-law out for lunch.

"No coffee shops."

"And?" I pinch my lips because I don't want to say it. "Daphne …" Ryan warns.

"Ugh, okay!" I shout. "For the next six months, I'll pretend I'm Claudia," I say, horrified. This is the worst concession I've ever made in my entire life – not that there have been that many – and Ryan makes me say it again and again. By now, it's pissing me off.

I've often wondered what Claudia does all day, and we've finally found out. It's all because of Arthur's loud complaining at family functions when he gets drunk – usually within an hour of arriving. He mostly grieves the recent loss of Glam, but he also complains about Claudia. It turns out, Claudia browses in the supermarket. She takes care to walk in the middle of the aisle at the supermarket, so she doesn't accidentally tear anything down. She's a nuisance to other people who're actually buying groceries for their families, but Claudia doesn't care. She also browses in the pharmacy. She browses in the waiting room of the podiatrist and other strange places. She's smart enough to stay clear of the retirement home, though, and she never buys anything anywhere. Hour after hour, day after day she just wanders about looking at things, taking care not to stumble while she practices swinging her hair discreetly. The White Ship to Grey Havens has definitely sailed for her.

"Good girl," Ryan says and gently kisses my forehead. I pretend I don't like it, but I do. He's the most caring and loving husband, and if he wants me to be lazy and do nothing while I'm pregnant, I'll try. At least a little bit.

"Don't say that. I'm not a dog," I complain because I'm angry and I need to complain about *something*.

"But you're *my* bitch," he says with a grin. I know he's only teasing me, but that's the *wrong* thing to say to a pregnant, hormonal woman.

"I'm not!" Before I know it, I clench my fist and punch him. There's a crack, and I freeze, completely terrified of what I've done.

"Bloody hell, Daphne!" he roars. Blood is pouring out his nose and down his shirt. He'll never be let onboard the plane like this. He pinches his nose and leans his head back.

"I'm sorry," I whine.

"Only because we'll miss the plane," he says drily. I promptly start crying – bawling's more like it – because I didn't mean to hurt him.

"I'm sorry." It's all my fault. We won't go to Amsterdam, and he'll lose his job. We'll be homeless, and our child will be born in the streets. We'll probably starve, too. God, the drama in my mind puts me closer to Claudia than I've ever been. That thought only makes me cry harder.

"So, at least that Krav Maga is paying off," Ryan says, strained. He's pinching his nasal bone hard, and the blood flow has already subsided slightly.

"I'm sorry." Ryan glances at me. He looks more tired than angry, and he's taking this much better than I deserve.

"I pity your martial arts dummy," he says with conviction.

"I didn't mean to," I whimper. Ryan sighs.

"Get me some tissue, will you? I need to change my shirt. I'm not going to Amsterdam wearing an 'I Love Manchester' T-shirt from the airport."

"But there's no time!" I whine. My lower lip starts quivering because if we miss the plane, it'll be all my fault. Ryan's career will be ruined, and he'll hate me forever. And that's all it takes for tears to run down my cheeks again.

Ticketholder for the Rollercoaster Ride

Ryan

"The plane leaves in five hours, Daphne," I admit tiredly. My wife might piss me off to no end, but I still don't like seeing her distressed. Truth is that Daphne's tears during the pregnancy so far have been mostly tears of fury. A hound of hell doesn't forget its origin easily, and neither does Daphne.

"What?"

"The plane. It's not until six."

"But you said ..." She's stopped crying – thank God for that – and her distress is replaced with confusion. As long as the confusion doesn't turn to anger, it'll be alright. *I'll* be alright.

"I know," I admit.

"Oh."

"I just ..." I sigh. "I just wanted some time in the airport with you without running to the plane like our lives depended on it." We've done that often enough. "I wanted a cup of green tea without burning my tongue. And I wanted to buy you something nice." Probably just toffee because Daphne's love of toffee became almost an obsession when she got pregnant.

"You want green tea?" Daphne asks sceptically. I bloody hate green tea, but when your pregnant wife has to forgo the Irishman whiskey and coffee and drink green tea instead, you can show some solidarity – at least when she's watching. At work, I guzzle coffee – even more than I usually do.

"Well, mostly, I wanted the rest of it," I admit. It would be nice if we got to the airport with time to spare. Daphne is never late, but it's a close call – every bloody time. She gives me that heart-stopping smile that makes me feel warm all over. God, I love her. I never imagined I could love that hellish creature, but I do. And I probably wouldn't love her if she wasn't so hellish.

"I'll get the tissue," she says and rushes out of the bedroom. I go to the mirror on the wall and inspect my face. It looks like I'll start my new job in a few days with a shiner. That's just perfect! Bloody Daphne!

When Daphne returns, I take the tissue and shove pieces into each nostril before I aggressively tear off my shirt. God, I'm pissed. That was not supposed to happen! I leave the shirt on the floor and head for the bathroom. When I look at my face in the mirror, I almost laugh. At least my broken nose isn't crooked this time, either. I've got to hand it to Daphne – her punches are very consistent, and at least I don't have to crack my nose back into place. I don't think a hormonal, pregnant wife would handle a roar of pain very well. Not even Daphne.

I carefully wash my face and chest free of blood. When I've changed the tissue in my nose, I almost look presentable. I have absolutely no idea what I'm going tell them at the airport, particularly not at security. Christ, this is a nightmare. Another nightmare courtesy of Daphne, the now hormonal hellraiser. I love her temper and her impulsiveness, but I also hate it. Especially right now. I take a series of deep breaths because none of us need me to fly off the handle. It won't end well.

Daphne is sitting on the bed when I return to the bedroom. She's wringing her hands nervously, and it makes me even happier I took a few minutes to calm down.

"Do you want me to stay home?" she asks timidly.

"Of course not," I scoff.

"But I just broke your nose again," she whimpers and stands up.

"I know." I turn my back to her and look in the closet. There's not much there, only a few shirts I never wear either because they're too small, too colourful, or just plain strange. That I Love Manchester T-shirt is starting to look awfully good. I sigh as I grab a patterned shirt. It's all things nautical – and pineapple. It's a hundred-fifty-pound Eton shirt Myles got me for Christmas a few years ago. Myles, the bloody coward, practically memorised the product description and rattled it off several times during Christmas – probably to convince our mother that he didn't mean it as a novelty gift, which he did. So, because Myles is the wimpy brother and doesn't want to admit that he simply wanted to annoy me, I can tell you that this sharp dress shirt features a micro print that is guaranteed to induce a smile or two. The versatile micro-printed shirt is unbeatable – adding interest to your look and starting conversations up close. Well, as long as it's about my shirt and not my bloody nose, it'll be alright. The shirt is lightweight, tightly woven and has signature Poplin for smooth, straightforward elegance. And it feels amazing putting on, by the way.

I finish buttoning the shirt and then turn to look at Daphne. My face hurts, I feel a headache coming on, and I'm pissed at Daphne. She's still my darling wife. She's still the mother of my unborn child. Unfortunately, she's also still a hellraiser.

"Then why don't you leave me here? I deserve it," she says quietly.

"Because," I say and look at her pointedly. "Regretfully, I'm *still* yours."

--- THE END ---

Thank you for reading "Regretfully Yours". I hope you enjoyed it, and if you did then please leave a review.

/B

More by B.L. Berg -→

Lady and the Tramp and Me

Life doesn't always turn out the way you think it should, does it?

For instance, what happens when you get a puppy you don't want? For Simon that answer is simply: nothing good.

His life as a happy bachelor is torpedoed when he reluctantly accepts a puppy of indeterminable breed who names himself Tramp and seemingly never ever stops growing – personality included. Any principles for raising a dog are put to the test, and so is Simon's state of mind when his sex-life is sabotaged, his sports car rendered useless, and Tramp is spending all of Simon's money.

And then there's the women… quite a few of them, but one in particular. The angry one in the park who likes dogs and who wonders if Simon is a stripper because he flashes her his ass. But in reality, he looks like he's just escaped from an asylum.

And that's just the beginning …

The Dream Maker and the Candy Cane

The truth is: Santa Claus is called Nicholas, he's an attention whore, and part of a Holy Trinity. The Christmas spirit is an old, grey cloud who is stoned most of the time. Santa and Mrs Claus aren't married, elves don't necessarily look like you think they do, and Rudolph is lost. Santa Claus needs bodyguards, teenagers are the true nightmare of Christmas, and Santa's opposition, Kram, is handsome as the devil.

Mrs Claus, Ivy, has a love affair with an elf called Noel – who really isn't that much into that Christmassy shit. Please remember not all elves look the way you think they do.

Nicholas, Ivy, and Kram are also keepers of the sacred universal balance and certainly, a single elf shouldn't be able to disrupt that and jeopardize Christmas – should he?

9 781917 367783